DO TRUST YOUR SPECIAL OPS BODYGUARD

Jewel Family Romances

CAMI CHECKETTS

COPYRIGHT

Do Trust Your Special Ops Bodyguard: Jewel Family Romance

Copyright © 2020 by Cami Checketts

All rights reserved.

No part of this book may be reproduced in any form or by any electronic or mechanical means, including information storage and retrieval systems, without written permission from the author, except for the use of brief quotations in a book review.

Editing by Daniel Coleman and Jenna Roundy

Cover art by Novak Illustrations

FREE BOOK

Sign up for Cami's VIP newsletter and receive a free ebook copy of *The Resilient One: A Billionaire Bride Pact Romance* here.

You can also receive a free copy of *Rescued by Love: Park City Firefighter Romance* by clicking here and signing up for Cami's newsletter.

CHAPTER ONE

Captain Isaac "Iceman" Jewel stared around at the exclusive, fancy party. They'd closed down one of the restaurants at the Jewel Resort on mainland Puerto Rico and invited only family and close friends to meet his older brother Joshua's girlfriend, Jade Jardine. The two had met here at the resort in November. It was now February. They weren't engaged yet, but Isaac was sure that was coming soon.

He smiled as he watched the couple, who were glued together as if separation would physically hurt them. Jade was a beautiful girl with long, dark hair and jade-green eyes. She and Joshua looked great together, but more importantly, his brother had finally learned to trust and let himself fall in love.

The twins, Seth and Caleb, approached him, and Caleb said in an undertone, "We found a stack of fireworks from the New Year's Eve party, big ones. You want to come with us to launch them over the heads of partyers on the beach?"

Isaac chuckled. These two were pranksters from the word

go. They'd both just turned twenty-five, and miraculously, Dad had given them each their five-million-dollar inheritance. Now he was probably questioning his sanity; who knew what they'd blow it on? Seth excelled at extreme sports—Bridger Hawk was his idol—and Caleb had proven himself a fabulous lacrosse player, playing in the NLL as an attack for the Denver Outlaws. It wasn't that they were wasting their lives, but they were just nuts. The trouble they'd gotten into as children, especially with being identical twins, was legendary in their hometown of Jackson Hole, Wyoming.

"I'll come watch," Isaac said, "as long as you promise not to aim at anyone."

Caleb wrinkled his nose as if considering. Seth stuck out his hand, the trademark blue Jewel eyes twinkling at Isaac. "Deal. See you on the beach in thirty, maybe forty. We've got to set up the show."

The two sidled off, laughing with each other. If only those two could each find an impressive woman like Joshua had. Maybe love would settle them down.

Isaac took a sip of his water and shook his head. Nothing would settle those two down. He'd better pray they found women who had a high tolerance level for "sturdy tricks" and lots of teasing.

Glancing around, he saw Mom, Rachel, and Eve smiling at something Paisley was saying or doing. Eve had run to Vegas and married some loser at nineteen. The jerk had left her shortly afterward. Each of the brothers had offered to hunt him down and kill him, or at the very least maim him, but Eve wouldn't even tell them his name. The only blessing of the union was Paisley. The three-year-old was hilarious and adorable. Isaac had told her once that she was spoiled, and she'd fired back, "Spoiled with lo-ove."

Dad and Luke were sitting at a table and talking intently, probably about some business venture. Most people would think they were arguing, but they were simply very invested in any conversation that involved business. Joshua had taken over Jewel Enterprises and was the billionaire catch of the group, but Luke wasn't far behind in net worth. Luke was an entrepreneur, always coming up with new ideas and using his inheritance to make them happen. More often than not, his ventures were wildly successful. Dad was his confidant and mentor, but definitely not his boss.

Isaac knew some of the people at the party, lifelong friends of the family, but there were others who were strangers to him. After graduating from Jackson Hole High, he'd spent the past eleven years working his way up in the Air Force, rising to the rank of captain and making his way into special warfare—special tactics of special reconnaissance, to be exact. He loved what he did and was proud of it, but he'd seen and done things that would make his mom cry at night if she knew.

He brushed the darkest memories away as his gaze lit on a beautiful woman. Her long, blond hair fell in soft curls around an angelic face. Her eyes were a deep navy blue, and her pretty bow of a mouth was pursed as she leaned toward her father. Cosette Peterson. It had been probably a dozen years since Isaac had last seen her, but he would never forget that beautiful face or how she had always made him smile with her funny, quirky personality.

During their teenage years, whenever their families would get together for vacation, he'd convince himself that he was in love with brilliant chemist Cosette. Nothing had ever come of it but one kiss that he'd never been able to put from his mind, on a beautiful beach in Costa Rica. Yet he'd been too wimpy to even ask her to text him. He'd joined the Air Force, and last he'd heard, she'd graduated with her doctorate degree, created her own line of perfume, her mom had lost her battle with cancer, and she was engaged to some wealthy guy who owned half of Vegas. A man would have to be a billionaire to think he was worthy of the likes of Cosette Peterson. Isaac scowled. He didn't care about money. He had plenty in the bank from his inheritance, and maybe someday he'd want to touch it. He lived just fine on his Air Force pay and was proud to serve his country. There was no reason to change his lifestyle.

Cosette's eyes swept the room and then landed right on him. Isaac felt himself straighten to his full six-two and expand his chest, even though he felt like he couldn't catch a full breath. As she stared at him, everyone else in the room disappeared.

Isaac gave her what he hoped was a welcoming, slightly cocky smile. If she was engaged, he shouldn't look at her like this, shouldn't feel this surge of desire rushing through him. He had to calm down and treat her like an old family friend, which she was.

He broke eye contact to check her left ring finger, but he couldn't get a clear shot from across the room. If only he had his sniper rifle. He smiled to himself, thinking how her overprotective father would respond to that. The Jewel boys had all been warned from a young age to keep their eyes and hands off of Cosette. It was ironic that Blaine Peterson thought Isaac and his brothers weren't worthy of his girl, since Isaac's dad was wealthier than Blaine and was also one of his closest friends.

When he focused back on Cosette's face, she was looking at him in concern, and her dad was whispering in her ear again. He wondered what had happened to her innocent, ever-present smile. She was a brilliant but spacey kind of girl, and he'd loved that nothing ever seemed to get her down. He'd really like to see her smile now. She looked insanely beautiful in a floral, summery dress, but she also looked like life had hurt her somehow. Probably because she'd lost her mom last year. Isaac couldn't imagine losing a parent, and Cosette and her parents were very close, as she was an only child.

A low whistle from nearby didn't break his concentration on Cosette. He knew it was just Luke, finally taking a break from "discussing" with Dad—or, more likely, Mom had broken them apart and reminded them it was a party.

"Loony Lovegood's even prettier as an adult, isn't she?" Luke asked in a quiet tone, referring to the nickname Seth and Caleb had given her from their favorite books, the *Harry Potter* series. Seth and Caleb also fancied themselves to be Fred and George Weasley—magicians, tricksters, and inventors.

"Yes, sir," Isaac said, staring unashamedly at her. Instead of smiling in response, she narrowed her eyes and turned to her father.

"I'm not your commanding officer," Luke teased him. "'My best-looking bro' will suffice when you respond to me." He gestured to Cosette with his glass. "Beautiful, but what happened to her smile and sparkle?"

"That's what I've been wondering."

"You gonna go talk to her, or just stare at her all night?"

"How long have I been staring?" Isaac rubbed the condensation off his water glass and kept staring. Cosette darted glances at him, but whatever she and her father were talking about must've been very serious, as she never once smiled. Was Isaac not enough of a draw to command her attention? Could he bring her smile and sparkle back?

"Long enough," Luke said. "Dad noticed and sent me to tell you to be a man and make your move instead of just staring at her all night. He's afraid if you don't reveal your honorable intentions soon, he's going to lose his oldest friend when Blaine challenges you to a fight and you have to kill him with your bare hands." There was laughter in Luke's voice. He was the closest to Dad, but their father was their champion. He thought highly of Blaine, but he'd always said it was ridiculous that Blaine didn't think his boys were worthy of Cosette. If his boys weren't worthy, nobody was, Dad used to say.

"That would be unfortunate," Isaac said. "That was a direct quote from Dad?"

"Yeah."

"Does that mean I have his blessing to pursue her?" Isaac pulled his eyes from Cosette's beautiful face to look around the room for his father. He was busy talking to Heath and Hazel Strong, Stetson Strong, and Jade's sister, Teal, who he thought was dating or engaged to Stetson, a Texas Titans player who Isaac loved to cheer for. His dad caught his eye and gave him a wide grin and a thumbs-up.

"I think that answer is yes," Luke said.

Isaac felt hope blossom in his chest. Finally. He looked at Cosette and found that she was focused on him again. She gave him a partial smile. Maybe it wasn't an invitation, but he was going to make it one. He'd march right up to Cosette and Blaine and ask permission to take her on a walk. Maybe Blaine had given up his stupid mandate and would finally approve of the Jewel brothers, most importantly of Isaac. But ...

"Wait!" Isaac whirled on his brother, who was grinning

openly at him. "I heard she was engaged. Mom told me that at Christmastime."

"Nope. She broke it off. You didn't hear this from me, but apparently the guy's family is Vegas mafia."

Isaac's eyebrows went up, and his stomach churned. He knew the rumors about Vegas mafia were true, no matter that the government wanted to claim they'd been shut down in the eighties. Why would an angel like Cosette get involved with someone like that, and how could Blaine have allowed it? She was a full-grown adult now, only a couple years younger than Isaac, so she'd be twenty-seven. Isaac knew that she was successful and independent, but from the looks of it, her father was still heavily involved.

From the looks of it ... His gaze swung back toward Cosette and her father, but they were gone. He cursed, shoved his water at Luke, and hurried across the room to where they'd been. The good Lord had seen fit to arrange for Cosette Peterson to cross his path again, and she wasn't engaged. Isaac wasn't going to miss out on this opportunity, even if her father did challenge him to a fistfight.

Cosette Peterson took one last long look at Isaac Jewel. She'd idealistically loved him from childhood on up. He'd only gotten tougher and more appealing with more years and experience under his belt. She could just imagine him with a sword taking on an entire squad of enemy soldiers, all of whom wore Vance Lansky's smug face. Isaac would cut her ex-fiancé down to size. She smiled at her silly musings. Her imagination was always going a million directions and she usually liked to live there, especially when she was creating fabulous scents in her lab, but Vance had zapped the happiness from her life and introduced her to ugly reality.

"Let's get you back to the room," her dad said quietly. He'd asked her to come to this party tonight to see his old friend's family. Cosette hadn't protested, as she'd hoped she might catch a glimpse of Isaac, but she was decidedly not herself and even on the best days she stank at social situations. All the perfumes and colognes in the room, added to the multitude of food and normal scents, had been a bit much for her ultra-sensitive nose. Her dad was still babying her, not wanting her to be uncomfortable. She wouldn't have minded so much if he wasn't taking away her view of the incredible Isaac Jewel.

She took her dad's elbow, and they walked out of the restaurant and through the resort. It was pretty quiet tonight, and beautiful water features decorated the spacious open areas. Would she see Isaac again before she left? Maybe they'd run into each other on a morning run. He'd be shirtless, and she'd stare in awe at that perfect chest, not even blinking or acting awkward. Maybe after her dad returned to the party, she'd go back to the beach for a walk and the good fairy would somehow bring Isaac across her path. A man like that could wipe away the awful memories Vance had created.

Pounding footsteps came from behind them. Cosette's heart raced, and she clung to her dad. "Somebody's coming," she hissed at him. Since she'd escaped Vegas and Vance, she'd lived in fear that he'd chase her down and hurt her.

Her dad darted a glance behind them and then patted her arm. He stopped walking and grinned. "Exactly who I hoped would chase us down."

"Excuse me?" She spun to see who her father was talking

about. Her heart rate increased when she saw the handsome Isaac Jewel racing their way.

Isaac slowed his pace as he approached. He looked incredible, filling out his dark gray suit to perfection. He was the darkest of all the Jewel siblings, with deep brown hair and naturally tanned skin. He still had the distinctive bright blue eyes. In most of his pictures that she'd seen over the years, he had been clean shaven, likely a requirement in the Air Force. He had short facial hair tonight, though; maybe he was letting it grow while he was on leave. She couldn't believe she'd ever thought the perfectly polished, perfectly conniving Vance Lansky was even attractive when there were men such as Isaac Jewel on the planet. Unfortunately, she was in no position to pursue her teenage crush. If Vance found her, she'd be dead, or at least she'd wish she was dead.

"Blaine, Cosette," Isaac said by way of greeting, sticking out his hand to her father first. They shook.

"Good to see you, son," her dad said. "You're looking fit."

Cosette was in a little bit of shock, and could swear the ground was moving. Why was her dad acting like Isaac was his long-lost son? When she'd been a teenager, her dad had forbidden her from dating any of the Jewel boys. Her face heated up as she remembered that one kiss she and Isaac had shared. Maybe her shock and the sway of the walkway were due to remembering that kiss and Isaac's bright blue eyes staring at her as if he'd just seen his first Bowie knife.

"Thank you, sir." Isaac was focused on her, though, not her dad. "Cosette ..." He said her name almost reverently. "It's amazing to see you." He extended his hand.

Cosette placed her hand in his. A warm surge traced along her palm. She bit at her lip and smiled at him. He was so handsome, she almost needed to shield her eyes as she looked at him. His blue eyes were as bright as the Caribbean Sea and just as warm. They held her captive, and she didn't want to ever look away. Her mind started conjuring all kinds of images of them playing in the sand and the water, walking on the beach late at night, stealing kisses. Ah ... heaven.

A throat cleared and Cosette startled, pulling her hand back and turning to her dad. He was grinning like the Joker, much to her confusion. What was her dad's plan, and why was he suddenly so happy?

Happiness had disappeared for her a few weeks ago. When she'd walked into her fiancé's suite to tell him she was calling off the wedding, she'd witnessed Vance carving into a man's back with a knife. Somehow, she'd been able to contain her screams of horror, silently slip away, and flee from Vegas back to her home in San Francisco. She'd reported it to the police, but the man had been "fine" when they'd checked on him, claiming that Vance hadn't hurt him, that he'd fallen mountain biking and "wrecked" his back.

She'd sent the five-carat diamond ring to Vance and broke up with him through text. His responses were belittling and threatening. She blocked his number and turned to her dad, who in turn reported the entire situation to the FBI. They took it more seriously and offered her protective custody, but her dad wanted to find the right person to keep her safe while he worked with the FBI to compile evidence against Vance. They'd flown to Puerto Rico to escape and he'd promised her the man they needed was coming. Could he be thinking ...?

As she looked into her dad's eyes, she felt a lurch in her stomach. "Isaac?" she questioned quietly.

Her dad nodded, and his smile tampered down a bit. He

whirled to Isaac. "How are you, son? How's the Air Force? Special ops, I hear?"

"Yes, sir. It's ... demanding, but it's the right fit for me."

"I can see that." Her dad clapped him on the shoulder. "Well, don't let me keep you youngsters."

Youngsters? Her dad was acting as nuts as most people claimed she was. Was she supposed to ask Isaac to protect her? She wasn't sure she was ready to spill her messed-up life to him, and she was pretty certain it was a bad idea for her to be alone with a man this appealing. She was still trying to wrap her mind around the fact that the man she'd thought she'd fallen in love with in a whirlwind romance in Italy a year ago was really a jerk who tried to belittle and emotionally abuse her and then revealed himself as a duplicitous gangster. She didn't need Isaac messing up her brain further.

Isaac smiled as if her dad had just handed him a gift. "Would you like to walk on the beach?" he asked Cosette.

A walk on the beach with Isaac Jewel. It had been a walk on the beach, without her dad's approval, that landed her a kiss with him last time. That kiss had inspired her views of romance throughout her sheltered life. She was mostly too busy in her lab and in her head with her creative ideas to notice real people besides her best friend Mar. Isaac had broken through, and she'd dreamt of his kiss since then.

Yet Isaac had never so much as asked to keep in touch. She'd assumed it was because she was "Loony Lovegood," as his twin brothers called her, or "Honey Lemon" from *Big Hero 6,* as his sisters had called her. She was socially awkward, and most people probably thought she was weird. It didn't matter. She had her friend Mar from middle school on up, and that was all she needed.

Except it had carved some happiness out of her when Isaac didn't pursue her. Over the years, she'd been able to somewhat push him from her memory. Now, here he was, a fully developed, tough, handsome man, and he wanted to "walk on the beach."

"I would love to," she heard herself say. She smiled and bit at her lip.

Isaac's eyes traced over her lips before meeting her gaze again, and she felt heat suffuse her face. He didn't say anything but offered his elbow. Cosette threaded her hand through his elbow and wrapped it around his bicep. The bulge of muscle there made her heart race and her throat go dry. How would it be to touch more of his perfect muscles? She blinked and tried to shut those wandering thoughts down. This was just a walk as old friends. Unless her dad was serious about hiring Isaac to protect her. Yet Isaac was still in the Air Force. He wasn't going to quit to be with her.

Her dad patted Isaac's shoulder again. Cosette wondered if Isaac was surprised by the change in her father. She knew he'd threatened many boys to stay away from her, including the Jewel brothers. When she'd gone away to college, she'd dated men—well, whoever Mar set her up with—and her father wouldn't have approved of most of them. She'd given up dating when she'd graduated with a doctorate in chemistry and started formulating perfumes. Her chemistry peers looked down on what she did, but she loved it. Scents were her obsession.

Speaking of, she leaned a bit closer and sniffed Isaac. Ah ... it wasn't one of hers, but she didn't mind the way his body chemistry mixed with 1 Million by Paco Rabanne. It was a nice mix of cinnamon, citrus, and leather. She'd love to try her Military Man line on him. It would probably be his signature cologne. She wondered if she'd created those scents with him in mind. There were always so many thoughts going on in her head that it was sometimes hard to pin down specific memories or inspiration. One that always stood out to her, though, was kissing Isaac.

"Have fun, you two," her dad said. "Take good care of her."

"Of course," Isaac answered seriously.

Cosette knew that her dad was concerned. They'd assumed from Vance's last texts that he'd gotten a tip from someone in Vegas's police force about what she'd seen and why she'd fled. He would probably try to find her. She'd at first assumed Vance wouldn't try to hurt her or "silence" her, but she didn't know anymore. Her innocent trust in mankind had been shattered. The sight of Vance carving up that man's back made bile rise in her throat and her hair stand on end. He'd been so callous and vicious as his men held the victim in place while the poor man let out the most heart-wrenching scream. She used to dream about new scents, fairies, and her mom up in heaven. Now she dreamt about that scream.

She forced her focus back to Isaac. Not that it was too hard with his strong frame close by and his handsome face tilted toward her with a secretive smile on his lips. He directed her away from her father as she clung to his bicep. Maybe she shouldn't have clung, but she was emotionally drained and his arm felt so good under her fingertips. They walked through the gorgeous resort, past the water features, and toward the pool areas and the beach beyond.

"Did you just sniff me?" he asked in a low voice close to her ear.

Cosette looked up. His face was right there. If she arched at all, she could kiss those tempting lips. Heat flared through her at the thought. "Hello to you too," she said back.

He chuckled.

Cosette pushed out a huffy breath. "And people claim I have poor social skills. I haven't seen you in ... at least twelve years, and the first thing you say to me is, 'Did you just sniff me?'" Sniffing people wasn't a socially acceptable thing to do, but perfectly mixed smells were her life's work. Of course she couldn't miss an opportunity to do a little practical research. Vance had refused to wear her Businessman line, preferring Caron Poivre at a thousand dollars per ounce. She thought the spicy oriental scent of Caron Poivre was a little heavy-handed, and it didn't mix with Vance's chemistry as well as her originals would have.

"And you're even more beautiful than you were twelve years ago, Cozy." Isaac's voice was deep, manly, irresistible. A smooth line like that from other men would have felt just like that—a line. From Isaac, it was the most beautiful compliment she'd ever received. She'd almost forgotten about his nickname for her. It had started off kind of silly: he'd told her that she was cozy and warm like a blanket when he'd impulsively hugged her once. He'd said it after he'd kissed her on the beach in the same husky voice he'd used just now. He made her warm, but definitely not "cozy"—more on fire.

"Thank you." She found herself leaning even more heavily into him. She wasn't tired around him—far from it, as he gave her a boost of energy—but she instinctively knew that he could lift and protect her. She needed both right now. So much. She'd lived the past few years in her lab, burying herself in creating delicious scents for her "Cosette" brand, naming them after different career paths for men and women and keeping the prices reasonable. Her best friend, Marietta, was a business and marketing genius. She'd worked countless hours and landed accounts with everyone from Target to Walgreens with her charming personality and vast network of associates. If Cosette wasn't going to be able to create in her lab until her dad determined she was "safe," it might kill her. How would they know she was safe? The only indicator she could think of was Vance being killed or arrested.

"You're even more handsome than you were twelve years ago, Ike," she admitted, also using the nickname she'd given him. Everybody else called him Iceman because he was cool under pressure, but he wasn't icy to her.

He smiled softly down at her. Had his eyes always been that blue, or had she forgotten?

They passed a myriad of pools, the water glowing blue in the night, and eventually made it to the soft sand of the beach. Other people were also strolling on the beach, and a few groups gathered together, most likely partying and drinking. Isaac directed her away from the crowds to where the beach was darker, more private.

She thought about taking her heels off to revel in the feel of the soft sand, but when Isaac stopped and turned to her, drawing their clasped hands up to his chest, she couldn't have cared less about sand between her toes. A thrill of anticipation and delight trickled over her as he used his other hand to brush a curl away from her cheek.

"Cosette," he murmured, "I—"

A sharp pop sounded, accompanied by an explosion of light. Cosette screamed and hit the ground, covering her head with her hands. Was this it? Had Vance found her, brought his henchmen, and now he was going to kill her and Isaac?

Tugging at Isaac's pant leg, she begged, "Get down! He'll kill us both!"

CHAPTER TWO

Isaac stared down at Cosette as she cowered on her knees in the sand with her hands over her head. She reached up and tugged on Isaac's pant leg. "Get down! He'll kill us both!"

More pops, whistles, and crackles came as fireworks lit the sky, some fired low over the water, some exploding over the beach or the resort. Seth and Caleb. Those two were going to hurt someone someday. It was a miracle they hadn't yet.

He bent down close and touched Cosette's shoulder. She was trembling. What in the world? He'd seen vets with PTSD who reacted like this to a sound like gunfire. What had happened to Cosette? Luke had said that her ex-fiancé was affiliated with the Vegas Mafia. Had the man done something to her to not only destroy her vibrancy and innocent smile but also terrify her? Isaac's gut tightened with anger at the man and concern for Cosette.

"Cosette?" he said softly. "Cozy? It's just fireworks. You're okay."

"Fireworks?" She glanced up at him, terror in her deep blue eyes. "Are you sure?"

He nodded. "Seth and Caleb told me they found a bunch left over from New Year's Eve and they were going to set them off. I'm sorry it scared you."

He reached out his hand. She took it and shakily let him lift her to her feet and wrap an arm around her waist. Normally, he would've loved having her close to him, if circumstances were different and she wasn't obviously terrified.

"Are you okay?" he asked.

She stared up at him. Her lips parted, and he hoped she would confide in him. He had almost another week of leave. He would happily spend that time protecting her, hunting down her slimy ex, and making sure the guy stayed far away.

"I'm exhausted," she said. "Do you mind walking with me back to my room?"

Not the answer he wanted. He didn't want to let her to go, and he really wanted to know why she'd react to a firework pop as if it were a terrorist with a machine gun. "Of course," he said.

Keeping his arm firmly around her waist, he walked with her through the resort and to the bank of elevators closest to her suite. She fit perfectly against his side. She was average height and came about to his chin. He wished his crazy brothers hadn't set off the fireworks and interrupted him. He'd been feeling pretty brave with her father finally acting like he approved of him. Isaac was going to tell Cosette that he'd always been interested in her. If it went well, he was going to kiss her like he had that night so many years before. Would her kiss now be as perfect as it had been then? All those plans had now been re-routed.

As they rode up in the elevator, he looked down at her and

said, "Cosette. What happened out there? Have you ... been in a bad situation?"

She harrumphed and stepped away from him, making his arm fall heavily to his side. Her sunny, happy personality had obviously been affected by either her mom's death, her life's struggles, or her loser ex, possibly all three. He wanted to help her stay safe and smile again.

The elevator opened and she strode out, not looking at him. Isaac caught up to her as she hurried down the hall to one of the large family suites. When they reached the door, Cosette pushed out a heavy breath. "I didn't bring my purse or a key with me. We'll have to knock."

Isaac rapped his knuckles against the door. "Why do you seem so disgruntled about it?"

"You know I love my dad, but it's been hard with my ... impulsive personality to convince him that I'm an independent adult and don't need an overprotective father anymore."

Isaac's eyebrows rose. He didn't blame her for wanting to be independent, and he had his own reasons for not wanting her father to be overprotective, but he also wanted to know what had happened to cause her to react to fireworks like that. She didn't seem inclined to tell him. It was one thing to be independent, but it was quite another to fall to the ground screaming when fireworks went off. She needed some help. He wished he could provide it.

Blaine swung the door wide and grinned between the two of them. "How was the walk on the ..." His voice trailed off, and concern filled his gaze. "What happened? Cosette, you're pale."

Cosette shook her head and pushed past her dad into the room.

Blaine glared at Isaac. "What happened?" he demanded.

"I'd better step in the room," Isaac said, keeping his voice level and calm as a vein was pulsing in Blaine's neck.

"I don't think that's a good idea. You seem to have upset my daughter."

"Dad!" Cosette said sharply. "All Isaac did was help me and kindly escort me upstairs." She lowered her voice. "Some fireworks went off and I … thought they were gunshots."

"Oh, Cosette."

Isaac looked at her dad. "Can I step in the room, please?"

Blaine stepped back. "Yes, please."

Isaac walked into the room, and the door closed behind him.

"Won't you sit down?" Blaine said in a muted voice.

"Dad, I don't think this is your best idea," Cosette started.

"Why not?" Blaine challenged her.

Cosette looked at Isaac, then out the darkened windows of the main room of the suite. She didn't answer.

Isaac walked over to the couch and sat, planning to be here for a while but not wanting to intimidate either of them with his large stature and military bearing. "At the risk of being impertinent, sir, can you please tell me what's happened that has Cosette diving for cover at a sound similar to gunshots? I'd like to help if I can."

Cosette's entire frame stiffened. She looked beautiful, tempting, and unfortunately closed off. She obviously didn't want Isaac involved in whatever was going on, but he needed to know who'd stolen her innocence, so he could kill them.

Blaine, on the other hand, appeared relieved and more than ready to share with Isaac. He sat down on the chair perpendicular to the couch and said, "Isaac, how much leave time do you have?"

"A week."

"Could I hire you?"

"Dad," Cosette reprimanded. She stormed over to them, staring deeply into Isaac's eyes. "Isaac. You are a very good friend of our family. We appreciate your service to our country. We think you're a fabulous, strong, brave, charming, and handsome man. Can you please leave?"

Isaac leaned back, surprised by her little speech. At least she still didn't have a filter, even if she had lost her sparkle.

Her dad stood and faced her. "He's the best choice. This man not only knows how to fight, how to protect, and how to watch for enemies; he obviously cares for you and will be a better bodyguard than anyone else we could find."

Isaac stood as well. "I appreciate the vote of confidence, Blaine, but you've never been the biggest fan of me or my brothers. Why the change?"

Blaine turned to him. "That's not true."

Isaac folded his arms across his chest and arched an eyebrow. If he was going to protect Cosette, they needed to get this out in the open first. Yet Cosette didn't want him. That stung.

Blaine splayed his hands. "When you were teenagers, you've got to admit that Caleb and Seth were crazy idiots, and the rest of you weren't far behind."

Isaac could give him that, but it bugged him that Blaine wanted to shove the past under the rug.

When Isaac said nothing, Blaine continued. "I was an overprotective fool, Isaac. Forgive me. As the years have passed, I've come to realize that the Jewel boys are some of the best I could trust with my girl—well, you, Joshua, and Luke. Caleb and Seth are still insane fools. I've also seen more and more that there are a lot of slimy snakes out there. Like Vance Lansky," he muttered under his breath. "I also have heard how accomplished, and well trained, you are from your time with the Air Force."

Isaac was probably duty bound to stick up for his younger brothers, but Blaine had a point. He wasn't sure how to respond, so he simply nodded and grunted, "Thank you."

"Please." Blaine gestured to the couch, love seat, and chairs. "Let's sit and talk this through. Cosette, please."

Isaac would do anything to help her. He stepped over to the couch but waited for Cosette to sit. Blaine watched her expectantly as well.

"Fine," she said through gritted teeth. "But I'm not a flighty little girl anymore. I am an adult, and you will treat me as one."

"Of course, love." Blaine gave her an indulgent smile. Clearly, he still thought she was twelve and should be wearing pigtails, not the form-fitted dress that showed exactly the kind of appealing woman she'd grown into.

Her words made Isaac strangely sad. He'd loved her flighty, impulsive, brainy scientist personality. Had she changed that much as an adult?

Cosette stalked over and sat on the opposite side of the couch from Isaac. He eased onto the cushions but stayed military straight. Blaine sat in the chair perpendicular him again.

"So." Blaine clasped his hands together. "I would like to hire you to be Cosette's bodyguard."

Isaac glanced at Cosette. She was biting at her bottom lip in such an appealing way that he had a hard time remembering all the questions he had for her. He did have to know, though. "Do *you* want me to be your bodyguard?"

Cosette's eyes slowly went over his upper body. "I'm sure you have more important things to do than follow me around my lab."

"Nothing is more important than your safety," he said, giving her a challenging look.

Her eyes widened.

"And he won't be following you around your lab," Blaine said. "You'll both take a small plane in the morning to an island nearby called Vieques. It's remote—no international airport, no cruise ships docking there. There are a handful of restaurants and stores, some resorts, but you'll be pretty isolated. I've rented you a beach house where you can enjoy a little ... vacation, while I work with the FBI and compile the evidence to get Vance arrested. Once that rat is taken care of, you can both go back to your lives." He spread his hands as if it were all that easy.

Isaac found he didn't mind the idea of a beach vacation with Cosette close by.

"I can't just ... not work!" Cosette said. "Who knows how long it will take you to take down Vance?"

"I'm sorry, love. You have no choice."

Cosette's nostrils flared. "I'm a successful businesswoman, and you will not hide me away in some beach bungalow."

Blaine stared at her, his blue eyes glinting. "I've already lost your mother. I won't lose you."

Cosette's fight disappeared faster than a popped balloon lost air. "I'm sorry, Dad."

He waved that away. "Please don't forget what that monster is capable, love. You saw how vile he can be."

Cosette shrank back against the couch and didn't say anything.

Isaac looked back and forth between the two of them. When no further information was offered, he said, "Can you tell me who this Lansky guy is and what he did to ..." He didn't want to say *mess Cosette up*, but ... "Hurt Cosette?"

"Vance Lansky is part of a very old mafia family based out of Las Vegas. The city officials thought they ended the mob's rule in the eighties when they had a 'black book' that barred all people suspected of having ties with organized crime from entering the casinos." Blaine smiled wryly. "The problem was, the mafia still owned most of the casinos under assumed names. There's been some new money coming in over the years, but it's mostly the old mafia families."

Isaac nodded, hoping the history lesson was over and he could get to what had happened to Cosette.

"Vance, of course, didn't tell Cosette where his money came from, or even what he owned when they met in Italy last year."

Cosette glared at the coffee table. Isaac's gut churned at the thought of Cosette in the arms of some slick, wealthy mobster. It wasn't just the jealousy he was fighting. Cosette was so pure and innocent; she would never suspect the evil some people were capable of.

"Their relationship was mostly long distance, but a few weeks ago, he asked her to come to Vegas for a week. She saw him torturing a man and escaped, of course calling the wedding off and informing the police."

Isaac's stomach now filled with acid as his neck prickled. He'd seen torture himself. He couldn't stand the thought of Cosette seeing it. "They didn't prosecute him for the man's death?" he asked quietly. Staying seated was difficult; he wanted to scoop Cosette up and hold her, reassuring her that he'd never let this Lansky loser touch her again.

"He wasn't dead," Blaine continued. "And when the Vegas police questioned the man and asked to see his back, he claimed he'd crashed on a mountain bike and ripped his back up on rocks." He shook his head. "The FBI are involved now.

Vance has been on their radar for a while, so hopefully we'll be able to find a charge that sticks. Vance's texts to Cosette were veiled threats before she blocked his number, so at least we have that."

"Such as?" Isaac hated to pin her down, but he needed to know.

Cosette spoke up. "Stuff like, 'I don't want anybody to carve up that beautiful face,' or 'How will your business recover when your lab explodes?' or 'How will you *live* without me? I don't think you will.'"

"Those aren't really veiled," Isaac grunted, his fists clenching. "And Blaine's right. You can't go back to your lab if he was threatening things like that."

"So you'll take the job?" Blaine asked.

Isaac nodded slowly, still studying Cosette. "I don't want your money, though."

"Spoken like a true Jewel man." They stood, and Blaine shook Isaac's hand. "All the arrangements will be ready for you to fly out in the morning. Eight a.m. okay? Sorry to take you away from your family."

"They'll understand," Isaac said. "Eight's fine." He turned to Cosette. "See you in the morning."

She nodded silently. The deep blue eyes that had once been so open and sparkling were now wary. She'd been damaged by a self-serving mobster. As Isaac strode from the room and headed toward the elevator, he wondered if he could somehow help her heal over this next week.

"Isaac?" Blaine called from behind him.

Isaac paused at the door, hoping Blaine would provide some extra insight into what Cosette had been through so he could help her. He'd seen damage like this, but he wasn't well trained in women's feelings, despite his feisty little sister Rachel trying her level best to help him.

Blaine stopped in front of him and didn't say anything for a moment. Finally, he looked right in Isaac's eyes and said, "I'm trusting you with my girl."

Isaac's eyebrows lifted. "I know, sir, and I plan to protect her."

"She tries to come across as this independent, tough businesswoman, but you know she's more a brilliant, spacey scientist. And I love that about her. I want to see her smiling and carefree again. What with losing her mom last year and thinking she was in love, then being tricked by this scum ..." He shook his head. "I just want my girl back."

"That's understandable, sir, but I wonder if you're not giving Cosette enough credit. Though she is a brilliant scientist, she's also grown into a capable woman and is running a successful business."

"I know." Blaine pursed his lips. "Can you please promise me not to lead her on with any romantic illusions?"

And here it was. Blaine still didn't think Isaac was good enough for his little girl. "She's not a child anymore," he said, folding his arms stubbornly across his chest.

"You don't think she's made sure I know that?" Blaine tapped his fist against his leg. "But you have to see that she's always had a ... crush on you, and she's vulnerable right now, not herself at all. Say she falls for you and then you leave for the military next week. That could damage her even more than Vance did."

Isaac startled. He would never willingly damage Cosette. He thought highly of her, and though he was attracted to her, he could see the wisdom in Blaine's reasoning. "I'm not going to do some irrational promise that I won't touch her or something like that," he said. "But I promise I'll be careful with her and considerate of her feelings."

"Will you wait until she's the carefree, happy Cosette before you pursue her?"

Isaac didn't like the way he'd been backed into a corner. He doubted that Cosette would be restored to her usual self before he left. Yet he didn't want to hurt her, and he certainly wasn't going to take advantage of her if she wasn't herself. "Yes, sir," he finally grunted out.

"Thank you for watching over her." Blaine shook his hand again and tilted his chin toward him. "Here's to me taking Vance down in the next week."

"I hope so, sir."

Blaine turned and strode away.

Isaac rode down the elevator to the main level, walked through the resort and behind the Italian restaurant to his family's private elevator. His family wouldn't like him leaving, but they all thought highly of the beautiful, smart, and adorable Cosette Peterson. They wouldn't blame him for offering to help her, though his more perceptive siblings might question how he thought he was going to survive on a tropical island with the woman he'd had a crush on for years.

Alone with Cosette on a tropical island. An hour ago, he would've thought it was a dream come true and his chance to finally charm the elusive angel, but he understood Blaine's concerns, and the last thing he wanted was to hurt Cosette. He'd focus on helping her, protecting her, and maybe starting her on the healing process.

Somehow, he needed to forget about their kiss. This was so much more important than his teenage crush.

CHAPTER THREE

Cosette went straight to bed after Isaac left. She didn't want to fight with her father. She knew she needed Isaac's protection, and she knew she needed to stay away from her lab. The knowledge didn't make it any easier. How was she going to go without working? How was she going to stay detached from the incredibly appealing Isaac Jewel when she knew she was in no position to give her heart away again? Vance had ruined her confidence by belittling her about the very things she knew she did wrong: no social skills, spacey scientist behavior, and no experience with romance. She wanted to find herself and her happy-go-lucky attitude again.

She woke at six and did a relaxing yoga workout. Maybe soon she could get back to running, the one break she gave herself from work. Would Isaac run the beaches with her? She liked the idea of that. If only she hadn't put herself in such a mess. She didn't want Isaac putting himself in danger for her. Yet if the well-developed muscles decorating his body and the success in the military his mom bragged about were any indicators, maybe she shouldn't be too worried about his safety.

Then she remembered Vance cutting that man while his burly bullies pinned the guy in place. Even Isaac wouldn't be tough enough to fight them off. Her stomach rolled as she imagined a knife carving into Isaac's strong back. No! She couldn't let herself go there.

Cosette packed her suitcase back up, fighting to clear her mind of awful thoughts. Sometimes it was rough to have an overactive imagination. She tried to eat some of the eggs, toast, and fruit her father had ordered for breakfast. The egg yolks were too runny, and the smell turned her stomach. Or maybe it was the memories of Vance, and the fear for Isaac, that nauseated her.

Right at eight, there was a knock on the suite door. Her dad rushed to the door, swinging it wide. Isaac's deep, lovely baritone floated into the suite. Cosette rushed the other direction rather than go hug him tight like she wanted to. After quickly brushing her teeth, she grabbed her large purse, shoved her laptop and phone inside, and swung it over her shoulder. Grasping her suitcase, she walked out into the main area.

Isaac was standing close to her dad, listening to his instructions. He looked incredible in a dark gray soft cotton T-shirt and black golf shorts. She recognized that she was not in a spot to pursue romance. She'd hardly dated outside of Mar's setups. The one time she'd let herself be swept away by a storybook romance, her fake hero had horrifyingly morphed into a conniving mobster. She didn't trust her own judgment where men were concerned. Yet she knew that Isaac was good and honorable. Truly, she wasn't worthy of him. Could she resist him? She'd have to pray hard that Vance did something horrible enough to get arrested. No, that was probably not a great prayer, as someone else would be hurt.

Isaac must've heard her, because he glanced up. She wanted to get closer so she could smell him. His bright blue eyes met hers, and they twinkled as he gave her a welcoming grin. The room was suddenly much too hot. Cosette fanned herself and saw her dad's brow furrow. She flipped her long, blond curls over her shoulder and tried to act unaffected. If Isaac could get to her with a simple glance, what was she going to do if he decided to use any other powers on her? Yet who was she to think a manly man like Isaac Jewel could even be interested? She was a silly girl whose attempt at independence had set her falling for the likes of Vance.

She walked to her dad's side and forced a brave smile. "You ready?" she asked Isaac.

"Yes." His gaze swept over her, appreciative, warm, and borderline sensual. Her dad was standing right here. What would Isaac do once they got alone? No, he wasn't that kind of man. It was just a look, and Isaac would never do anything inappropriate. His family was as religious as their Biblical names.

She turned to her dad. "Thank you for watching out for me. I love you." She felt guilty that she'd been so obstinate last night about him being overprotective and her not being able to work. She was the one who'd brought this trouble on her and her family because of her flighty, impulsive nature and willingness to trust anyone. Her dad was just trying to protect her. She knew that. And she knew how much he loved her, especially with the love of his life gone. Her mom's loss had left a huge hole in their family.

Her dad smiled softly at her. "It's going to be okay, love. Isaac will keep you safe and I've got the contacts and the resources to bring Blaine down."

"Be safe, please," she whispered as she hugged him tight, savoring his scent of musk, vanilla, and cloves. It was her "Seasoned Man" line, and she'd created it just for him.

Her dad chuckled as if he were the Air Force special ops tough guy. "I'm not worried about me." They hugged for maybe longer than Isaac was comfortable watching, but this was her dad and he needed to know that she loved him, especially if Vance somehow got ahold of either of them. She couldn't let her imagination go there.

He released her and gave her a gentle nudge. "Trust Isaac. It's going to be okay."

Isaac gave her dad a nod and then took her suitcase and gestured her out the door. Trust Isaac? She didn't know how to get back to that innocence.

"Love you, baby girl," her dad said.

Usually, the title of "baby girl" would bug her a little bit, as even though she knew she was childlike compared to most women, she also liked being the spacey yet sassy scientist. She and Mar had created an internationally renowned company. Mar had helped her learn how to be proud and confident. Right now, she was feeling like a lost little girl who missed her mom and her best friend, and she wished she hadn't let her guard down and let the slime Vance in.

"Love you," she returned.

The door fell closed behind them. Isaac picked up a large bag and tossed it over his shoulder, clutching her suitcase with the other hand.

"Thank you," she murmured, starting for the elevator. Isaac followed close behind. Once they were in the elevator, she became intensely aware of his scent. He smelled good. She could make him smell better.

Neither of them said much as they descended the elevator, walked through the gorgeous property and lobby, and then stepped up to the waiting car out the front doors. The driver loaded their bags and ushered them into the back seat but didn't start a conversation, as if he could sense the tightness between them. Cosette didn't like it. She'd always enjoyed being around all the Jewel family, particularly Isaac. Though she'd had far too many silly romantic fantasies about Isaac, she'd still thought of him as a good friend. Now, they had nothing to say to each other.

Ignoring the driver's slightly smoky scent, she focused on the new car smell. She glanced back at the picturesque resort and said, "Do you hate leaving it? It's prettier than Cinderella's castle."

Isaac looked out the window as well, then back at her. He shrugged. "I hate leaving my family, but the resort is just a place. I've been in too many impoverished situations to get too caught up in the luxury of my family's resorts."

Cosette wanted to hear all about those situations, but not while the driver was obviously listening in. She simply nodded and looked out the window, clueless as to what to do about the tension growing between them. Mar would be proud of her for even sensing it. Social cues were not Cosette's specialty, and she was constantly begging her best friend for interpretations and suggestions.

When they reached the international airport, they thanked their driver; Isaac offered him a tip, which he refused, saying that it had been included. They had to check in through airport security and then go to a separate area for private planes. As they walked outside again and across the tarmac to the waiting white Cessna, the warm air teased her hair and the air smelled of jet fuel and hot asphalt. She asked, "Are we flying in one of my father's planes?"

He shook his head. "We don't want Lansky to have any way to track you. I asked Joshua if we could borrow a plane, and of course he said yes."

"You and Joshua are still close?"

Isaac nodded. "Besides my team, he and Luke are my closest friends."

"What do you think of Jade?" Cosette had thought she was fabulous and wished they could be friends. She had mostly had imaginary friends growing up as an only child and living inside her own head so much. Marietta had found her in middle school, but nowadays her friend was busy running their business and couldn't be with her every minute. Cosette missed her.

"She's perfect for him. He needs to be sassed more, and she's a natural tease." Isaac smiled tightly, but then he stopped fifty feet from the plane and looked her over. "How close were you to Lansky?" Isaac asked in a gravelly voice.

"Really close the week in Italy, Christmas in San Francisco, and a few weeks ago in Vegas," she admitted, wondering why they had to talk about that right now. "Besides that, we communicated through FaceTime the past year."

Isaac set down his bag and released her suitcase. He held out his hand, and she stared at it. He wanted to hold hands with her? She wouldn't mind, but was now really the time for that? They needed to get on the plane and get to the safe place; then they could discuss awful things like her and Vance. Would they have time to discuss happier things like Joshua and Jade? She craved happiness like she used to know before Vance.

"Cell phone," he demanded.

Cosette had a sinking feeling in her gut, but she pulled it out and handed it to him.

He looked it over briefly, then pulled a small tool out of his pocket and pried it open. His mouth was pressed in a grim line as he looked over the battery. Replacing the tool in his pocket, he didn't snap the phone back together; he took it and hurled it at the pavement.

"Jiminy Christmas!" Cosette screeched, looking down at her ruined phone. How was she going to keep in contact with her employees and business contacts without her phone? She couldn't remember the last time she'd gone a day without talking to Mar. She gripped her purse tightly. If he tried to do that to her laptop, she would fight him. Not that she stood much of a chance against his mass of muscle.

Isaac looked at her. "I'm sorry. There was a tracking device in your phone."

Cosette put a hand to her neck, suddenly feeling exposed and vulnerable. Her gaze darted around the private jets lined up. Could Vance or one of his men be watching her even now?

"Don't worry." Isaac put a hand on her arm, and its warmth brought comfort and a thrill of pleasure. "I haven't seen any signs we're being followed. I doubt he's following you yet. No reason if he knows where you are, right? He'll get concerned when it stops reading, and even more so when your dad goes after him. This is the perfect place to have it stop tracking. We could be flying anywhere in the world."

He ground the phone under his heel, then picked up the pieces and chucked them at a nearby fence. They scattered around and settled on the asphalt. Gesturing toward the plane as if he hadn't just destroyed a thousand-dollar phone and her lifeline to her business, he picked up his bag and her suitcase handle.

"What if he figures out what plane we were on?" she asked.

"If he somehow connects our families and finds the plane, the flight plans have the plane landing on Dominican Republic, the second most populous Caribbean island. He'll have a time following us there. The stop in Vieques won't be logged."

Cosette hated to say it, but she had to ask. "Do you think he'd have tracking devices anywhere else?"

"Was he ever alone with your purse or laptop or anything like that?"

She shook her head. "The only time he had my phone was when I first met him in Italy. I went to use the restroom, and he kept my phone to put his number in. I was stupidly thinking it was romantic, but he must've had a tracking device on me for the past year." The thought made her sick. Vance had obviously been planning to control her from the very beginning. Her dad had wondered if their first meeting was coincidental, or if Vance knew exactly who she was and wanted the resources her company and family money could bring him. It wasn't enough that he had family money and plenty of wealth on his own.

Cosette just wondered why a man couldn't love her for her. Besides the threatening texts, Vance had also told her how she'd never find someone who loved her, as she was socially impaired, crazy, and kissed like a limp noodle. Despite Mar's vehement protests, Cosette knew his jabs were probably true.

"Looks like it. If that's really the only time he had your phone."

She searched her memory and nodded. "I think so."

They reached the plane and were greeted by the pilot. Cosette was glad there wasn't a stewardess—that meant there was less worry of someone talking to Vance's men. Was she paranoid for thinking he was coming after her? The tracking device was unnerving. Settling into the seat, she found her gaze lingering on Isaac's strong build. He seemed to know his stuff and was built like the Terminator. If anyone could protect her from Vance, it would be him. If only she could be reassured that Vance and his men wouldn't find and torture Isaac. She'd never forgive herself if that happened.

CHAPTER FOUR

Isaac alternated between staring out the window at the beautiful scenery flowing below and staring at the beautiful woman seated close by. She was going through something rough, and he was now her protection detail. If only he could keep his mind from noticing every detail about her, from the way she bit at her lip to the way she splayed her fingers occasionally, as if reminding herself not to clench them. He couldn't even let himself think about how it felt to touch her, or he'd slide down a rabbit hole that would have them cuddling close in the beach bungalow until her dad pinned down Lansky and Isaac got the chance to make things right. He liked the idea of holding her close, once he'd settled the score with Lansky.

When she stretched her fingers wide and pressed them against her thighs for the dozenth time, he asked, "Why do you do that?"

"Do what?" Her navy-blue eyes darted to his, and he felt a

little stitch in his chest. He rubbed at it, hoping he wasn't getting sick.

"Stretch your fingers out. Do they hurt?"

"Oh." Cosette looked down at her hands and gave a soft laugh. "No. I spend a lot of time typing on the computer and clutching vials in my lab. A doctor recommended I stretch them whenever I think of it, so I don't get arthritis or carpal tunnel or something like that. I do it so often I don't even realize it. It bugged Vance. He'd kiss my fingers and say they were too pretty to be getting damaged by chemicals." She snorted in derision and clasped her hands together.

Isaac's brow furrowed. There were some burn marks on her fingers, but he didn't mind them. He wished he could kiss them and tell her they were beautiful—but he didn't plan on doing anything similar to what Lansky had done, and he was already forgetting that he shouldn't get involved with her romantically. "I think it's amazing what you've created," he said instead. "I have no idea how you can create scents like you do."

"Thank you. I think you have some idea, though. If I remember right, you and your brothers were always building bombs."

Isaac laughed. "That was mostly Seth and Caleb, and what you do is infinitely more impressive than building bombs."

She shrugged. "It's all chemical reaction, right?"

"I guess so." He smiled at her. "I've never known a chemist besides you, and you definitely don't fit the stereotype."

"What do you mean?" Her lips pursed.

"I imagine someone crazy like Doc Brown in *Back to the Future,* or someone all intense like Severus Snape in *Harry Potter.*"

Instead of laughing, she stiffened and looked away. She used to be so impetuous and adorable; now she seemed sad and withdrawn.

Isaac swallowed, not sure what he'd done wrong. He touched her arm. "I didn't mean to offend you."

She glanced back at him, her eyes suspiciously bright. "It's okay. Vance pretended that he was thrilled with my career at first, and then he started mocking me about it, calling me his 'mad scientist.' His latest texts told me how I was straight-up crazy."

This Vance guy had no right to call Cosette his anything, but Isaac didn't really have that right either. "Why were you ever with that loser?" he asked quietly. He hated hearing about any kind of romance involving her with someone else, but especially with a loser like Lansky. He'd researched the guy last night. He was a cocky prick.

She didn't meet his gaze. "When we met in Italy, I was researching for a new line and he swept me off my feet. It was a whirlwind romance, and then we went our separate ways. We communicated through FaceTime and text for about a year. It shocked me when he came to visit me in San Francisco for Christmas and asked me to marry him. He convinced me he was in love, and I said yes. I'd never had someone in love with me before."

Isaac's eyes widened at that. She was beautiful and brilliant and used to be a lot of fun. What man wouldn't want to date someone like Cosette?

"When he brought me to Vegas ... I saw what he was really like." She shuddered.

Isaac thought about what she'd seen. Could he help her heal

over the next week, restoring her smile as well as protecting her? For the first time since he'd been appointed to special ops, he wished for more leave time. He always enjoyed his leave and his family, but he had a higher purpose and was always ready to get back to doing his part to keep the world safe.

The jet approached a small airport, and minutes later, they were touching down. He appreciated that Cosette had opened up to him, and he could easily see how someone innocent and sweet like her could be tricked by a predator like Lansky. He still hated thinking about it.

Cosette walked through the gorgeous beach bungalow, breathing deeply of the salty breeze floating in from the ocean and the fresh smell of Pine-Sol from the cleaning ladies. The retractable walls in the main area were open, and the view was unreal. The bungalow was elevated on stilts, and the living area's openness showcased the view of a beach lined with palm trees and an ocean as blue as Isaac's eyes. It was a large room with a well-stocked kitchen and living area. Two bedrooms with a shared bath were off to one side. Though it was obvious the builder had spared no expense, it was intimate and ... cozy. She smiled, thinking of Isaac's nickname for her.

Now if she could only figure out what she was going to do with herself for the next week. Kiss Isaac and test different cologne samples on his skin? Hmm. Both of those would definitely have a reaction of some sort.

Cosette walked out onto the large patio. There were some comfy-looking outdoor sofas, but she was too restless to sit and enjoy the sea air. She eased down the stairs and onto the sand.

Taking her sandals off, she dropped them by the stairs, wound through the palm trees, and out onto the beach. Taking in a long breath of the salty air, she let the sun kiss her face. She stretched her hands out wide and said aloud, "Thank you, Lord, for your beauties. Please help me find my sunshine again and put the darkness behind me."

Finishing her prayer, she sauntered westward. They were on the north side of the island, on a beach that was supposed to be private. Looking around, she definitely didn't see any intrusive neighbors. She loved the populated but beautiful beaches of San Francisco, but there was definitely a different feel to this tropical, soft-sand beach.

As a definite workaholic, Cosette spent a majority of her days in the lab and was used to being alone. Even though she itched to work, she thought she might be able to get used to seclusion like this. Especially if one handsome military man was here.

"Where are you going?" Isaac's voice came from her left.

She whipped around and put a hand to her throat. "Don't scare me like that with your sturdy tricks. I'm liable to have a heart attack."

He smiled. "You're too young to have a heart attack."

She wagged a finger. "It's happened."

"I can't believe you remembered about sturdy tricks. Seth and Caleb were so full of it."

"They still are." When she'd spent time with their family as a child, Seth and Caleb were always playing "sturdy tricks" on everybody, especially her, because she reacted so dramatically. She cast a casual glance at Isaac, and she really liked the way his gray shirt draped his muscular build. "I was just going for a tromp on the beach."

"I have to be with you at all times." He shrugged. "Sorry about that."

Cosette's eyes narrowed and she put her hands on her hips, ready to tease with him. "My friend Mar explained to me that when someone says, 'Sorry about that,' they're basically saying, 'I don't give a rat's behind.' Did you know that?" Cosette was constantly asking Mar to explain expressions and social situations to her. Mar kept reaffirming that Cosette was fun and perfect and did just fine, but Vance's belittlement rang in her head and made her doubt all the confidence she'd gained over the years.

"I didn't." Isaac chuckled softly. "'A rat's behind'? Such vile language."

She arched her eyebrows. "I'm sure you've heard much worse."

"Sadly, I have." He tilted his head. "You want to 'tromp'?"

"Yes, thank you."

They walked slowly, with nowhere to go and plenty of time to get there, as her mom would've said. She missed her mom. Hoping to take her mind off of that, she asked, "How on earth are you going to be with me 'at all times'? That doesn't really work, you know?"

Isaac pumped his eyebrows. "Who says?"

A warm flush came over her. She might have been too innocent, but she wasn't stupid. "You're sleeping in your own room," she shot at him.

"How about if I sleep on your floor?"

Cosette gasped. "You're joking."

He shrugged and gave her an infuriating smirk. "Slept in worse spots."

"Do you really want to be by my side at all times?" she

demanded, refusing to allow herself to imagine him sleeping, especially close by her. Even though she pushed the image from her mind, her body still felt too warm.

His gaze moved carefully over her, making her shiver with a pent-up desire she hadn't known she had stored inside. She'd thought she loved Vance, but for the most part their relationship had worked because he'd pretty much left her alone and was over-the-top romantic when she saw him. She knew a relationship like that would never work with Isaac. He'd want her, every inch of her: emotionally, physically, and spiritually. Isaac was the complete package, and he'd expect his woman to give him everything as he would give her everything—his time, his love, his devotion—until he'd left her for the military again.

She had to look away so he didn't see how much she wanted to be his everything.

Isaac stopped walking, and she drew herself to a halt as well. He tilted her chin up and stared deeply into her eyes. Those blue eyes of his were powerful and seductive. "I would love to be by your side at all times," he said in a husky voice that pulsed through her.

"But you have to go back to the military next week," she heard herself remind him. Ah, dang it. Her tongue always got the best of her. Way to kill the mood. Not that she should be letting herself have "moods" with Isaac. He was her protection. Her dad would take care of Vance, and she'd go back to her regular, busy life, creating new scents and working with Mar to make sure the marketing and production teams were doing their jobs. Life would be good—and boring. Yet she'd seen what a mess romance could bring into her life. Even though Isaac was a good man, there was no guarantee that romance with him would end any better than it had with Vance. Okay, at least she'd never see Isaac torture someone and she wouldn't literally run from him, but maybe a spacey scientist wasn't destined to find love. Her scents, her best friend, and her dad should be enough for her.

Isaac's eyes shuttered and he stepped back. "You're right. And somehow I don't think you'd work as a leave fling."

"Excuse me?" She cocked an eyebrow at him and folded her arms across her chest. "You've had ... 'leave flings'?" What in the world did that mean? Mar would probably pick it up instantly, but Cosette was lost.

Isaac's jaw tightened. He looked like he wanted to lie to her, but she knew that wasn't in his nature. He finally shrugged and said, "I've dated women while on leave. When I go back to base, the relationship fizzles out and dies. Nobody really wants to deal with a long-distance relationship."

A roar of jealousy flickered in her. Oh ... flings with women while he was home. She could count the number of men and boys she'd kissed on one hand, and Isaac was one of them. It wasn't hard to imagine women crawling all over Isaac. "And why wouldn't I work as a 'leave fling'?" she asked.

Isaac studied her carefully, and his eyes became a smoky blue. "Because a girl like you is meant to be loved and cherished, not deserted."

Cosette could only blink at him as her heart stuttered and then resumed its pace at a frenzy. Would Isaac love and cherish her, or was he only speaking in a general sense? It was a compliment, to be sure. Except ... girl? Did he think of her as a girl, or as a woman?

She had to ask, "Would you have to desert me, then?"

Isaac's tongue moistened his lips, and Cosette found herself leaning closer. He smelled clean today, less like his cologne. She alternated between staring at his lips and his blue, blue eyes. "I would," he admitted in a gravelly tone.

Cosette jerked back as if he'd slapped her. Apparently, she was to be "loved and cherished," but not by him. It shouldn't sting so bad, yet she knew she'd probably never be loved and cherished by anyone. She was too flighty, too spacey. Men didn't settle down with the brilliant chemist. Especially not tough, perfect men like Isaac.

She forced a smile and hurried off down the beach. Isaac caught up to her and trailed along. Neither of them spoke. A week in a cozy beach bungalow might not be so ideal if it was going to be like this. She tried to remind herself that she wasn't in the market to date, not after the last nightmarish experience. It didn't help, as all she wanted to do was pin Isaac down and kiss him, but if Vance was right, she stank at kissing and Isaac would leave her regardless.

Her irrational dreams with Isaac couldn't happen, so she just kept walking.

"Do you want to race?" Isaac asked, cocking an eyebrow at her.

"Excuse me?"

"Race. If I remember right, you used to love to run, and dance, and pretty much be adorable."

Adorable. So Isaac did think of her as a little girl. Dang it. A studly man like him would never want to kiss a little girl. It was fine. "Let's go," she challenged. She pushed off and sprinted down the sand.

Isaac laughed loudly behind her and then took up pursuit. Cosette gave it her all, arms pumping, legs rotating as fast as she could make them go. She wasn't as fast as she'd been as a teenager, but she still ran every chance she got and sprinted at the end. The warm wind rushed past her face, and she reveled in the beauty of this stretch. The soft sand cushioned every step, and the view of palm trees to her left and the ocean to her right was gorgeous. She could smell salt, wet sand, and some unfamiliar earthy plant scent. Sprinting in such a perfect locale was glorious. She had fabulous running routes in San Fran, but all of them were crowded with people, and none of them had a handsome man chasing her.

She could hear Isaac's footsteps pounding behind her. Her heart was already racing from the sprint, but when she imagined him catching her, sending them tripping and getting all tangled up together, it thumped out of control. Gasping for air, she risked a glance over her shoulder and found that he was almost upon on her. His face was a mask of determination, and his body was a walking billboard for tough military man. His muscles worked in synchrony as he sprinted. They were long and lean, and she just wanted to touch one ...

She tripped on who knew what and rolled through the sand.

"Cozy!" Isaac yelled. He was instantly upon her, helping her to a seated position and studying her with concern. "Are you okay?"

Cosette pushed her hair out of her face and patted at her arms and abdomen. "Everything's still here." Her heart rate was still elevated, but that was to be expected from that sprint, not to mention the warm way this incredible man was staring at her. Could she yank him down to the sand and roll around for a while? No, that might be socially inappropriate. If only she could call Mar.

Isaac chuckled. He shook his head and brushed some sand off of her face. "Adorable," he murmured.

Cosette didn't need the reminder that he thought of her as a precocious child. She struggled to her feet, and he grasped her elbow and helped her up. "Do you concede defeat?" she asked, tossing her long hair back.

Isaac grinned. "Never."

She wrinkled her nose at him and took off sprinting again. His deep chuckle reverberated behind her, and he quickly took up pursuit. Cosette laughed and upped her pace. Even before the Vance debacle, she'd been getting far too serious and finding less enjoyment in her work or running or even being with Mar or her dad. She honestly couldn't remember the last time she'd felt this free and happy. Isaac might not be interested in her as a woman. She could convince herself that she wasn't ready for romance anyway. It was enough she could feel like herself again, at least for the moment.

CHAPTER FIVE

Isaac stepped out of the shower, humming as he got dressed. He and Cosette had sprinted for a long time, taking breaks to walk and talk, and then one or the other would issue a challenge and off they'd go again. Once they'd gotten back to the house, he'd offered to let her shower first. She'd teased that he needed the shower more, as she still smelled like her incredible perfume. He grinned at the memory. She smelled so good at all times, and it was driving him to distraction. Yet it was nothing on how great she looked or how she made him smile.

In the end, she had showered first, and he'd busied himself with burpees, push-ups, and planks to try to keep his mind off of that water running. He'd told her dad that he'd be sensitive and give her time to heal. Yet she already seemed more like the carefree Cosette he'd loved as a teenager. Maybe a simple getaway, and being away from this Lansky jerk, was what she needed.

Isaac walked out of his bedroom and into the main area. He

breathed deeply, drinking in the scents of grilled meat, peppers, and onions. This sealed it. She was pretty much perfect.

Cosette was dressed in red shorts and a white tank top. She turned from the stove, which faced a view of the many trees on three sides of the house. She grinned and said, "I hope you're a hungry hippo, because I cooked a lot."

He just stared at her. She was so beautiful with that long drape of blond hair, her deep blue eyes, and her smile. How was he going to resist her until she was healed? How would he know she was healed? Was it fair to fall for her when he knew he was leaving soon and there was no hope of them being together for the long term? His enlistment was up next year. Would she wait for him? That was crazy thinking. He wasn't ready to retire or move to a desk job. He loved what he did. He thought highly of Cosette, but that was all. They weren't in love. They had no commitment of any kind. Twenty-four hours ago, they hadn't seen each other since they were teenagers. She probably didn't even think of him as anything more than a friend. Yet the way she looked at him told a different story.

Right now, she was looking at him as if he was hurting her. "You don't like fajitas?" she asked.

Isaac pushed out an unsteady laugh. "I love fajitas, and I'm starving. Thank you."

Her smile was restored, and she flipped some tortillas on the griddle, then turned back to the stove to stir the meat and veggies.

"Is there anything I can do to help?" he asked.

"Sure. Look in the fridge and find cheese, sour cream, anything you can find to go with them."

"Okay." Isaac rushed to do as she'd asked and found the fridge was fully stocked. He pulled out salsa, sour cream, grated cheese, and some avocados. After he'd sliced the avocados and set the rest on the small table, he found plates and silverware and grabbed a water bottle from the fridge for each of them.

Cosette brought the meat, veggies, beans, and tortillas over. They sat down at the table, and when she reached out to him, he clasped her hands. Her touch sent a surge of warmth through his whole body. He bent his head and waited.

"You say it, please," Cosette requested.

"Sure." Isaac said a brief prayer of gratitude and requests to watch over their families and bless the food. They both said amen and then started assembling fajitas.

Isaac took his first bite and moaned. The veggies, beans, and meat were seasoned and cooked perfectly, and the tortillas were fresh. The salsa, sour cream, cheese, and avocados added to the delicious combination of tastes, but the fajitas would've been amazing even without them. "Are the tortillas homemade?" he asked.

She smiled. "Yes."

"Are there recipe books around here? I destroyed your phone, so I know you didn't Google a recipe." He took another bite while he waited for her to answer.

She shook her head, nibbling at her own food. "I don't need recipe books."

"Why not?"

"Cooking is just another chemical experiment, right? My mom taught me the basics when I was young, and now I just experiment within that frame of reference."

Isaac's jaw went slack. "That's incredible. What else can you cook?"

She wrinkled her nose at him. "I'm a renowned chemist and I

create bestselling scents, and you think it's 'incredible' that I can cook without a recipe?"

"You're brilliant, I know that," he hurried to say. "It's definitely more incredible that you've created the lines of perfume and cologne. Forgive me for being a man and thinking with my stomach."

She tilted her head, and that blond sheen of hair fell over her bare shoulder. Isaac forgot all about the delicious fajita he was gripping as his mouth went dry and something warm stirred within him.

"You're forgiven," she said. "But you're dripping fajita juice out of your wrap."

Isaac hurried to set his fajita down and blot the juice on his leg. "Sorry."

"Stop apologizing." She smiled at him and took another bite. "Thinking like a man, eh? What else would you like me to cook?"

Isaac used his fork to spear some of the peppers and onions that had slid out of his wrap onto his plate, and he thought of how lucky he was to be here with her. "I'm not picky. I'll eat anything if you're willing to cook it."

"Don't you cook?"

"No. I'm either eating military cafeteria food, MREs when we're on assignment, or takeout or restaurant food when I'm with my family."

"I forgot your mom doesn't cook."

"Yeah." He shrugged. "She's great, and I'm not complaining, but home-cooked food is my favorite thing—well, next to my M4 Rifle."

Her brow furrowed at that, and he realized his mistake. She'd seen something horribly violent, and from what he remembered, she'd never been a fan of weapons.

"Sorry," he said.

She waved that away. "So what are your favorite foods?"

He thought about it. "If I tell you, you don't have to make them. You don't even have to cook. Just because I love food doesn't mean I want you slaving in the kitchen while we're here."

She smiled wryly at him. "I enjoy cooking, and it gives me the chance to create, since I can't be in my lab."

"You miss your lab?" he guessed, munching on his fajita.

"Horribly, but ..." She gestured at the beautiful landscape outside. "This isn't torture." Her smile slipped as soon as she said the word "torture."

"I wish I could take away what you've seen," he said before he could stop himself.

She watched him, her deep blue eyes serious. "You've probably seen worse."

"Maybe, but I signed up for it."

She bit at her lip. "Nobody should have to see that—or worse, have it happen to them."

Isaac agreed.

"Does it get better?" she asked, her lip trembling.

"Yes," he said. "You don't forget it, but with a lot of prayer, talking with the right person, and sometimes professional help, it stops being the first thing you think about in the morning, or the thing you dream about at night."

She considered that for a moment and then picked at another bite. They ate quietly for a while, and Isaac waited for her to either talk more about what she'd seen and what she feared, or move on.

"So what are your favorite foods?" she asked.

Isaac smiled at her. She was resilient, but he'd still like for her to talk about the trauma she'd been through and get it off her chest. "I remember your mom made us homemade bread and potato soup when we came to visit you in San Francisco once. That's a taste I've never forgotten."

If she was bothered by his reference to her recently departed mother, she didn't act like it. "Mom's bread was amazing." She paused for a moment and then said, "Do you have things to do this afternoon, or are you going to sit and stare at me as I cook?"

He'd happily sit and stare at her, but he admitted, "I need to set up some perimeter security."

Her gaze sharpened on him. "Do you think he'll come after us here?"

"No," he said. "It's just precautionary."

"Okay." She smiled bravely. "You get going on that, and I'll cook."

He smiled too. He could get used to this arrangement.

Cooking had always soothed Cosette, and she busied herself in the sunny, open kitchen, making bread, potato soup, and chocolate chip cookies before throwing a salad together. It was a little odd to be cooking soup and bread when an eighty-degree breeze was flittering around her from the open-air house, but she thought it was very sweet that Isaac had remembered her mom cooking for his family. Cosette could think of dozens of times that her mom had made this same meal for her and her dad. She missed her. Her mom had loved and embraced Cosette's impulsive, flighty nature. She knew it worried her dad.

All of her work that afternoon proved to be worth it. When Isaac came in, he reacted to the smell of fresh-baked bread with over-the-top gratitude. They carried a comfortable conversation as they ate, talking about what each of his siblings were up to. After dinner, they cleaned up side by side, he kept thanking her for the delicious food. She accepted his praise, but she wanted to ask him if he still thought she was "adorable," or if the fact that she could cook and bake had made him realize she was a woman, not the whimsical teenager she'd been. Yet she liked her whimsical side, even missed it. The terror of Vance and the loss of her mom had pushed it away. Being here with Isaac restored it. If only she knew he didn't think of her as a child.

The sun was dipping toward the west as they finished cleanup, and Cosette wasn't sure what they'd do with themselves. There was no Wi-Fi here; she'd checked, but her computer hadn't worked. Maybe they could watch one of the DVDs she'd seen stacked by the television or play cards or something. She felt restless just thinking about sitting around and watching a movie.

"Do you want to walk on the beach?" Isaac asked.

"Oh yes, please." She clapped her hands together and beamed at him.

He smiled and gestured to the opening for the door.

"Will we close all the glass tonight?" she asked. She might have a hard time sleeping otherwise. The bedrooms and bathroom had normal walls and windows with shutters, but the main part of the house was so open with the retractable walls that it was almost unnerving.

"Sure," he said.

They eased down the porch steps and through the palm trees, walking quietly along the beach in bare feet. She wondered how far this stretch of sand extended. "Could we run in the morning and see how far we can go?"

"You really like to run, don't you?"

"Yeah. It's the only break I take from work."

"So you're pretty much a confirmed workaholic?"

She nodded. "Pretty much."

Isaac glanced down at her. "That's crazy. The Cozy I remember was a lot of fun."

"Life kind of knocks the fun out of you." She frowned but changed the subject quickly. "You and your brothers used to call me Loony Lovegood."

Isaac chuckled. "No," he corrected. "Seth and Caleb called you that, but they fancied themselves Fred and George Weasley, so I wouldn't put much stock in what they said."

"What did you call me back then?" she asked.

He smiled secretively. "Cutie Cozy."

She wrinkled her nose. Cutie? Definitely a childish nickname.

"Don't you like it?" He shifted closer to her as they walked.

Cosette inhaled at that moment, and she sighed and leaned closer, taking a long sniff of him.

"Did you just sniff me?" Isaac asked.

Cosette tossed her head impertinently. "So what if I did? Smells are my life."

He laughed. "So what do I smell like?"

"1 Million by Paco Rabanne," she answered without missing a beat. "It's a mix of cinnamon, citrus, and leather. It works well with your body chemistry, and I'm sure the average woman would think you smell nice."

"That's impressive. You not only recognize my cologne but know the scents in it." His eyebrows rose, but then his brow furrowed. "Wait. You don't think I smell nice?"

She shrugged and said in a challenging tone, "You could smell better."

Isaac stopped and turned to her. "How's that?"

She couldn't resist smiling at his frustration. "You do smell 'nice', but I have a few cologne samples I'd love to try on you. I think my Military or Athletic lines would blend perfectly with your body chemistry, and then you would smell ... irresistible."

Isaac's blue eyes seared into her. The sun had dipped and the night was falling, but those eyes still had plenty of light in them. "Would I be irresistible to you?"

You already are. She swallowed and managed to say, "Come on, let's go play with scents." Tugging at his hand, she turned toward the house.

Isaac followed along, and luckily, she didn't have to answer his question.

They got back to the house, and she sat him down at the kitchen table. "Okay, wait here while I get samples and some supplies."

"This sounds serious." There was a teasing glint in his eyes, but she didn't feel like he was downplaying her career; he was just teasing her. He made her feel light, like she was her old, happy self again.

"It is. Don't move." She winked at him.

"I wouldn't dare." Isaac chuckled and splayed his hands. The muscles in his biceps flexed as he did, and Cosette felt a little unbalanced.

She hurried away to her room, grabbing a small bag of samples. She found a clean washcloth and wetted it, then grabbed a handful of cotton balls and a bottle of hydrogen peroxide. Returning to the kitchen, she smiled when she saw that he hadn't moved from his seat. "Okay, are you ready for this?" she asked.

"To be irresistible to you? For sure."

Cosette's breath caught in her throat. Was he interested in her as a woman? She still felt like damaged goods from Vance, but she was betting one kiss from Isaac could restore her. Her face flushed. She couldn't let herself think about kissing Isaac, or she might obsess about it nonstop. If only she could call Mar for some advice.

"Okay." Her voice was shaky as she sat down close to him, piling the supplies on the table. "First, we need to clean off your cologne."

He nodded, his gaze not wavering from her face. Cosette's hands trembled as she put some hydrogen peroxide on the cotton ball and leaned in close, dabbing at his neck with it. Isaac's pulse thrummed visibly. When she glanced up at him, his blue eyes held her captive and she froze for a second. If she moved just a few inches, their lips would align, and she could see exactly what his lips would do to her.

Vance's taunts about her horrible kissing ability rang through her head, and she broke from Isaac's gaze and picked up the wet washcloth. She softly rubbed it across his neck a few times, not letting herself meet his eyes again. "Do you, um, put your cologne anywhere but your neck?"

"I spray it on my shirt," he said in a husky voice.

"Oh." The implication washed over her. This wouldn't work if he had cologne on his shirt. Unless he ... "Oh!" Her face flared hot, and she couldn't meet his eyes.

"Do you want me to take it off?" There was laughter in his voice now.

Cosette's gaze darted up to his again. He was smiling at her, but instead of a twinkle in those blue eyes, there was a mixture of mischief and desire. She felt none of the mischief but all of the desire.

Without waiting for her to respond, Isaac pulled his shirt over his head and dropped it on the nearest chair. Cosette gasped and stared. The muscles in his arms, shoulders, chest, and abdomen were ... delectable. They were defined and thick and so tempting that she lifted her hand and almost touched his rounded pectoral muscles before stopping herself. She was breathing heavily, and she couldn't meet his gaze or test scents on him like this.

"You need to put a shirt on," she said, her voice trembling. Was she revealing exactly how awkward she was?

The silence stretched between them. Both of them were breathing much more quickly than was normal for sitting at a table. The only other sounds besides their breath was the breeze rustling the palm tree leaves and the water rolling onto the sand —no crashing waves here. Cosette's gaze darted outside then dropped to the table. She couldn't bring herself to look at Isaac or ask again.

Isaac didn't say a word. He stood and walked to his bedroom. Cosette let herself stare again. The muscles in his back were just as impressive as the front. As he pulled the door open and his arm muscles flexed, the breath whooshed out of her. He glanced over his shoulder at her, and she almost fell off her chair. Had a man ever been that appealing, that perfect?

Once he'd disappeared, she leaned back in the chair and took slow breaths. Where was Mar when she needed her? Mar might tease with her about her lack of exposure to the male species, but she'd patiently answer Cosette's questions about what to do with these feelings. Yet Isaac was so much more than some man to her, and she wanted to experience these feelings with him.

Isaac walked back out of the bedroom, and she averted her

gaze and opened her samples bag. He sat down, his knee brushing hers. "Cozy," he murmured.

She forced herself to meet his gaze so he didn't think she was a complete wimp. He'd pulled on a blue T-shirt, and she admired how it complemented his eyes and showcased that chest she'd gotten a glimpse of.

"I'm sorry," he said.

"Sorry?" Giving her that glimpse of his perfect chest was nothing to be sorry about. It wasn't his fault she'd reacted so awkwardly.

"You're so innocent and pure. Have you never seen a man's chest before?" he asked quietly.

Oh, great. They were back to him thinking she was a child. She was confirming it with her overreaction to his beautiful shape. "Well, I, um ... yes!" she got out with exasperation.

His gaze said he didn't believe her. "Then why did you react so ... intensely?"

"I've seen chests, all right, at the beach and pool and stuff. I'm not some innocent simpleton." She blew out a breath, not wanting to tell him why she'd reacted the way she had. They were on day one and might be here for many more. How in the world was she going to survive without attacking him?

"When I said innocent " he began.

"No, it's fine." She held up a hand, not wanting him to kindly explain how she'd acted like a child. "So, let's try out my Athletic Man scent first."

"All right." He didn't say anything more about her reaction or tease her about her lame "innocence." As he leaned closer, his warm leg brushed hers again, and warmth sparked in the pit of her stomach. At least he was wearing a shirt now. That helped temper the desire ... no, it really didn't.

Focusing on her colognes, she unstopped the vial and put some on her finger. She started talking in what she hoped wasn't a nervous rattle. "The base note in my Athletic line is a woodsy citrus scent with top notes of ginger and musk balanced by a wave of fresh grass."

He smiled at her. "Thank you for the description."

She forced a smile in return and lifted a trembling finger to his neck. He held still as she smeared the cologne down one side of his neck and then the other. She didn't let her fingertip linger on his skin. Pulling her hand back, she avoided his gaze as she stood and hurried to the sink to wash her hand.

When she returned and found him staring up at her, she knew there was nothing for it. "I'm going to have to ... sniff you now."

His eyebrows went up as he gave her a slow grin. "Okay."

Cosette took a steadying breath. She stayed standing but leaned down to his neck and inhaled deeply. She liked the freshness of the scent but wasn't certain this was *his* scent. Even though he was obviously athletic, he was a military man clear through. She was saving that one for last.

She straightened quickly and said, "It's good—fresh and clean. It would definitely work for you, but ... let's try again."

"Not irresistible yet?" he asked, smirking.

"Not quite." She smiled, hoping he didn't see how he affected her. Taking the cotton swab with the hydrogen peroxide, she rubbed off the scent, then wiped him clean again. It was a beautiful torture to be this close to him. She wanted to sit on his lap, show him that she knew how to kiss and wasn't a child. Her mouth turned down. She didn't know how to kiss. Her experience was limited: she'd kissed Isaac as a teenager; a guy she'd dated briefly in college—she thought his name was Mace, maybe

Jace; some man Mar had set her up with after college, Tom; and Vance, who'd told her only a few days ago that she was an abysmal failure at kissing.

Cosette pulled out a different vial and held it aloft. "Okay, this is my Businessman line. One of my top sellers for men, actually. Its base note is the tang of pineapple, with top notes of bergamot and blackcurrent. Powerful, simple, and tantalizing." She tried to pump her eyebrows but was unnerved by his proximity, and she kept imagining him with his shirt off. Dang her overactive imagination.

He laughed. "You should do commercials."

"Yeah, that would go over well."

He cocked his head and said, "I think you'd be amazing on commercials."

"No thanks, I'll stick to my lab. Mar takes care of all the other junk I don't want to deal with."

"Mar's your business partner?"

She nodded. "Best friend, business partner, marketing extraordinaire. She's the best."

"Is she okay without you?"

"I'm sure Mar doesn't need anyone." Mar didn't have any family or any close friends besides Cosette. Men flocked to her door and she enjoyed dating, sometimes going on multiple dates per day. She loved Cosette and always claimed she needed Cosette's brilliance, imagination, and positive attitude. Cosette was aware that if she hadn't developed her scents, Mar wouldn't have a product to sell, but sometimes she thought that Mar could sell dirt and people would line up to buy it.

"Are you okay without your work?"

She shrugged. Today had actually been fun. That seemed crazy, as they were hiding out from her psychotic ex, but being with Isaac was all she'd hoped for and more. "I'm fine." She put some cologne on her finger and then gently ran it over each side of his neck, taking it slow and savoring the feel of his smooth skin and his pulse thrumming under her fingertip. Luke, Caleb, and Seth all wore beards, but Joshua and Isaac were usually clean shaven. She liked beards, but she liked feeling Isaac's skin and seeing his handsome face even more.

Pulling back, she rushed to the sink to wash her hands again. When she turned, she saw Isaac standing and stretching. Her pulse raced and she stayed next to the sink.

He walked over to her and leaned in close. "How do I smell?"

Cosette shut her eyes and breathed him in. "Delectable," she said, before she could stop herself. Her eyes flickered open.

Isaac was leaning closer to her. He slowly, tantalizingly brushed her hair over her shoulder, his fingers doing a number on her sensitive skin. He bent down and sniffed her neck, then slowly exhaled against her throat. "Delectable," he murmured.

Cosette laughed uneasily to hide the thrill she felt as his warm breath rushed over her skin. "My Imaginative Woman line. A sweet and feminine fragrance gives each woman a sunny outlook, with iris, jasmine, and orange blossom at its heart, juicy pear and blackcurrant at the top, and patchouli at the base. An unashamedly girly perfume for day or evening wear."

Isaac chuckled. "Yes, you should definitely do commercials."

She bowed slightly.

"I'm a fan," he said, leaning closer still. "It mixes *perfectly* with your body chemistry."

Her stomach whooshed as if she were on a roller coaster. "Th-thank you," she murmured.

Isaac watched her with eyes full of longing. Cosette had never felt so desirable, even with the man she'd thought was going to be her husband. She recognized now that Vance was all wrong, but she still shouldn't be so taken with Isaac so quickly.

She pulled away and strode around him. "Yours is not quite there, though. Let's try the one I think will be our winner."

Isaac lifted his eyebrows at her, as if challenging her for daring to walk away from him. Wowzers. The powerful military man was irresistible.

She ignored the look and gestured to the chair. He slowly walked in her direction, his gaze never leaving hers. What did he want? A kiss? She put a hand to her throat and knew that her limited experience with men had failed to prepare her for the likes of Isaac Jewel. Could anything have prepared her to be alone in a tropical paradise with a man so ... manly? She realized now her little perfume game was playing with fire. She shouldn't have suggested it. She should stop now.

Isaac sat. She automatically cleaned off his neck and heard herself saying, "And finally, I think this will be the winner: my Military Man line." She didn't tell him that she'd had him in the back of her mind as she created this one. "This cologne is a combination of deep basil, warm spice, and brushed suede. It defines casual elegance and strength while exhilarating the senses with a blast of fresh air for the man who was meant to protect and serve." She gulped as she finished and Isaac gave her a heated look.

Isaac leaned closer in his chair, tilting his chin up so she had full access to his neck. She gulped and put some cologne on her finger. Slowly, she raised her shaky finger to his neck and dragged it across. He swallowed as she did, and for some reason, his neck moving under her fingertip filled her stomach with a flash of heat. Her hand moved to the other side of his neck, and her finger lingered on his pulse, which sped up.

Cosette pulled back, and their gazes locked. She couldn't have moved if a bulldozer was coming at her.

"So you think this is the one?" Isaac asked quietly.

She thought *he* was the one. "Um, we'll have to give it a minute for the alcohol to evaporate and mix with your body chemistry."

He nodded. "Anything I can do to speed the process?"

"Warm air helps. I could blow on it." Her eyes widened as she realized what she'd said. Oh no!

"Yes, please." He gave her a smoldering look that she felt clear through.

She should not do it. She should not lean in and blow on his neck. Instead of heeding her brain's promptings, she leaned in so close she brushed against his chest. Feeling unstable, she braced herself, grabbing on to his far-too-perfect muscular arms.

She glanced up at him. He was breathing more quickly, and his blue eyes were concentrated on her. What was she supposed to do? It took half a beat of staring at him before his delicious scent invaded her brain and she sighed. Blow on his neck. That sounded ... appetizing.

She felt like she was floating as she leaned against his broad chest, clung to his arms, and exhaled on his neck. His body shuddered against her. Was he feeling what she felt? Hot, breathless, full of anticipation? Was there anything wrong with moving just a bit closer and pressing her lips to his neck? She couldn't think of anything, so she did.

Isaac let out a soft groan as her lips connected with the warm skin of his neck. She heard herself groan as well. She wanted to trail her lips up his neck to his face and see what kind of a reaction kissing him full on the mouth would do to the both of them. Inhaling deeply, she said against his neck, "It's perfect. You're absolutely irresistible."

"To you?" he asked in a husky whisper.

Cosette's mind was foggy, distracted by his delicious scent, the desire she felt for him, the warm look in those blue eyes. Isaac was all she'd ever wanted, and she was finally right here with him, and unless her social radar was even further off than she'd feared, he was giving every indicator that he wanted her too.

A loud beep sounded from Isaac's pocket. He jumped, cursed, and stood quickly, moving around her while he pulled his phone from his pocket. "Get in your bedroom and lock the door," he commanded.

Terror rushed through her. What was happening?

Isaac was focused on his phone. She ran for the bedroom, shutting and locking the door behind her. As she leaned against the door, her heart raced out of control. Her gaze darted around at the large windows that she'd thought were so charming, facing the thick trees next to the beach. Now she wondered if Vance and his bodyguards were going to burst through those trees, grab her and Isaac, and start cutting them up.

Her breath was coming faster and faster, and she thought she was having a panic attack. She'd never had a panic attack. What did they feel like? She wanted to Google symptoms, but she remembered that she had no Wi-Fi on her computer and no phone. She felt lost, alone, terrified. Where was Isaac? What was happening? How would she know to come out of the room? What would she do if Vance hurt Isaac?

Pressing her palms harder against the door, she forced herself to remember her mom's advice throughout her life. She bowed her head and begged for help: *Please protect Isaac. Please.*

"Cosette?" Isaac's voice floated through the door.

She whirled around and yanked it open. He looked great, perfect. She flung her arms around his neck and squeezed him tight. "You're okay? Is Vance here? Did he cut you?"

Isaac chuckled. "No one's here, and your Vance isn't going to hurt me."

Cosette pulled back and muttered fiercely, "He's not *my* Vance."

"Noted." Isaac raised his eyebrows and gestured out into the trees. She felt so exposed with all the retractable doors open, though she might not feel much better with them closed. Anybody could hack through glass, right? "It was actually a pig that set off the alarm."

"A pig? Like a wild pig, or somebody's pet, or somebody's dinner?"

He smiled at her. "A wild pig. He was big, big enough to trip the sensors. We're safe. Since we're elevated like this, no animal is going to get in, and nobody else is out there."

"I think we should close the wall things now."

"Okay."

They busied themselves closing and locking the retractable walls. When they finished, Cosette wanted to recreate the moment, but she had no clue how. Dang being socially inept. Dang not having a phone to call or text Mar.

She grabbed the cotton balls, hydrogen peroxide, and washcloth and motioned to the colognes. "You can keep the samples."

"Thanks." Isaac walked to the table, stopping just before her.

They'd been so close when the stupid pig had tripped the alarm. Now she had no clue what to do. No matter Mar's reassurances to the contrary, it was obvious from her experience that she was a child when it came to romance and hunky men. Isaac was out of her league, and he would probably laugh if he knew her immature longing for him.

"Good night," she murmured, hurrying to her room. Glancing back, she saw him watching her with those blue eyes that made her want to stare at him all night long.

She shut and secured the door behind her, hoping and praying that she could sleep. The scare with the alarm was one thing. The appealing look in Isaac's eyes was quite another.

CHAPTER SIX

Isaac spent a restless night. He didn't know what was happening between him and Cosette, and he wasn't sure if he should let it happen. He'd told her dad ... what had he told her dad? That he'd wait to pursue her until she was more herself, or something to that effect. But she seemed plenty like her adorable, fun self. She was the one who'd sniffed him, put cologne on his neck, blown warm air on his neck, kissed it with her warm, full lips. His stomach lurched as he thought of that, and he wanted to go back to that moment, minus the interruption of the alarm.

Cosette was so innocent and refreshing. Even the terror of her ex hadn't stamped out those qualities in her. Maybe that was his cue that she was all right and ready to move on. With Isaac. Yet it hadn't been long since she'd been with the jerk. Maybe Isaac needed to honor her dad's concerns and slow down. He was only here six more days. He needed to go back Sunday. He was currently stationed out of Hurlburt Field, Florida, in a beautiful base on the panhandle. He didn't have a deployment scheduled, but he could guess that one was coming. How could he treat Cosette like she was another "leave fling" and kiss her and then walk away? He couldn't, and he knew it. Yet he couldn't give up his career for a relationship that wasn't even a relationship. If only he knew how to resist her in this close proximity. The problem was he had no desire to resist her.

He woke early and went out into the main area. The sun was cresting the eastern sky, and the sea shimmered in the kiss of the morning light as it filtered through the trees lining the beach. Those same trees crowded in on their all-window main area.

He drained a bottle of water and wondered how long Cosette would sleep. She'd wanted to run this morning. A long run would hopefully help him relieve some energy and frustration, but he doubted it would help him not kiss her if they got close like last night again. All the reasons not to were getting very fuzzy in the face of how adorable she was.

Her door opened, and Isaac whipped around. She stretched and yawned as she walked out. Her hair was sticking out at odd angles, and her eyes blinked rapidly. With her too-short cotton shorts and a tank top, she looked far too appealing as she stretched. The bottom of her tank top rode up and showed some smooth, creamy skin.

"Oh!" She gave a cute little gasp and immediately dropped her arms, as if she knew exactly how it affected him.

"Good morning," Isaac said.

"I'm not so sure about that." She covered another yawn with her hand.

"Did you not sleep well?" He hadn't, but that had everything to do with the beauty in front of him.

"No. You?"

"Not really," he admitted.

She gave him an impertinent look with her eyebrows lifting and her lips tilting up. Did she know exactly why he couldn't sleep? Was she feeling the same? "Sorry about that," she said.

Isaac chuckled, remembering her saying that "sorry about that" basically meant you didn't give a flip. He would implement that expression with his buddies.

"You ready to run?" she asked.

"Sure, if you are."

She didn't say anything, simply turned back into her room and returned a half a minute later with her hair in a long, smooth ponytail and her running shoes on.

"You always run in your PJs?" he asked.

She shrugged. "I'm not picky about what I wear for much of anything. Mar buys me dresses when we have to go to events, and either comes over with a heap of clothes, or helps me dress through FaceTime, when we have meetings with people who she thinks matters."

Her answer showed impressive confidence and reflected her innocent and carefree personality. It was good she had a friend she trusted, but Isaac hoped that this Mar wasn't controlling Cosette. Cosette needed to be free to be her unique, fun self.

He waited while she took a long drink from a water bottle, and then they walked outside together. The freshness of the sea air touched his skin, and he filled his lungs with it. It was still too warm in his opinion, probably mid-seventies, but it was a beautiful spot of earth.

They started at a slow jog along the firm sand down by the water. "So you care about how you smell but not so much about how you look?" he asked, remembering how cute she'd been last night chattering about base notes and top notes like this adorable infomercial. He startled as he realized that he'd never thought anyone was adorable before, besides his niece Paisley. Cosette was all woman, yet she still managed to have that fresh adorableness about her.

He noticed she hadn't responded to his question besides pulling in a quick breath.

Isaac glanced at her. "You okay?" he asked.

She nodded quickly and increased her pace. Isaac hurried to keep up. He tried to ask her questions as they ran about her schooling and creative process, but he only received one-word or one-sentence answers. He'd offended her somehow. What had he said?

They cruised along the beach for four miles, according to his watch, and then turned back. Sweat was dripping down his face and back. The sun rose quickly, and it was hot out here. He looked longingly at the ocean. If he'd been with his buddies or brothers, he'd rip his shirt off and dive in. Cosette's reaction to him taking his shirt off last night confused him. In a way, it made him smile, but it also concerned him. Maybe she was afraid of strong men. The photos he'd seen of Lansky online showed a polished, preppy loser, not a tough guy, but who knew?

They arrived back at the beach next to their house. Cosette didn't say anything to him, but she plopped down on the sand, untied her shoes, pulled them and her socks off, and shoved her socks in her shoes. Isaac stopped next to her, staring down at her shape. Her legs were very nicely formed, and with her shorts riding up slightly, he was having a hard time looking away.

Still saying nothing, she pushed up to her feet and waded into the water until she was waist deep and then dove under. Standing again in the water, she flung her hair back and swirled her hands in the ocean.

Isaac just stood there, staring at her in breathless wonder. He appreciated that she'd go swimming without worrying about a stylish swimsuit, but the problem was how her tank top draped against her fit body.

She looked at him, squinting at the sunshine. "Do you want to swim?"

"Oh, um, yeah ..." He was reminded again of her intense reaction when he'd taken his shirt off last night. He didn't want to swim in a shirt, but he wanted her to be comfortable around him. Pulling off his shoes and socks, he waded into the water.

"Goodness' sakes," Cosette sputtered, staring at him. "You can take your shirt off."

Isaac stopped in the knee-deep water. "I didn't want to ... you were so shaken last night by it."

Cosette's mouth pressed into a line. "I'm sorry. It's fine. Take your shirt off. I just won't look."

"Okay." Isaac pulled his shirt off and tossed it at the shore.

He pushed through the warm water and then dove under. They swam out for a ways and then treaded water. It felt great, except that Cosette studiously avoided looking at him.

"You could look at me now, since I'm under the water," he said.

"Oh." She forced a smile. "Yeah, that's right." Finally, she turned her gaze to him.

"So you have issues with men's chests?" he asked.

"No!" she protested, narrowing her eyes at him, or maybe it was just bright out here. "I just don't want to be ... ogling you as if you're a piece of meat because you're so beautifully built and stuff." She clamped her mouth shut and swam away from him. "I'm going to go shower and start breakfast," she called over her shoulder.

Isaac wanted to follow her, but he didn't. She thought he was beautifully built? He wished he could tell her exactly how beautiful she was. As she waded through the water and the tank top and shorts clung to her nicely shaped body, he made himself look out at the ocean. She'd said she didn't want to ogle him, and he felt guilty because he definitely wanted to ogle her.

He pushed a hand over his face. This week was going to be a long one.

Cosette rinsed out her clothes and hung them on hooks in the bathroom, then took a long shower. She wanted Isaac to take her seriously as a woman, yet she couldn't even look at his bare chest. And he thought she cared about how she smelled but not how she looked? That was unflattering. And then there was the way he'd been facing out at the ocean treading water as she turned to look before she climbed the porch steps. If a man wanted a woman, wouldn't he be checking her out every chance he got? She knew a relationship shouldn't be based on physical attraction, but there should be attraction, right? She sighed. She and Isaac had no relationship beyond him being a family friend and offering to protect her. She should stop blowing things out of proportion, as she often did when it came to people and their unexpected reactions. Chemical reactions were more reliable.

She got dressed and put on minimal makeup. Isaac had said that she didn't care about how she looked, and that was hurtful, though she didn't think he'd meant it to be. Of course she cared; it just wasn't her focus like a lot of other women she knew. She admired women like Mar for taking such good care of themselves, but shopping and makeup were like a foreign language to her. At least she tried. She exercised, ate right, and used some of the makeup Mar had helped her buy when Cosette had begged for help one day. She dressed a lot more simply than someone like Mar, who was always dolled up and dressed to impress with her spike heels, but Cosette had hoped that Isaac might like a simpler woman. It didn't look like it. He kept calling her "adorable."

When she exited the bathroom, he was waiting. His shorts were wet but not dripping, and his chest was ... bare. Cosette steeled herself. She could do this. She could stare at his beautiful chest, check him out, and not act like a child about it. Taking her time, she let her eyes slide over his muscles and languidly make their way to his face.

His blue eyes twinkled with amusement, and he was smiling broadly at her. "Ogling?" he asked.

"Ah!" she gasped. "I tried *not* to ogle. You tell me what I'm supposed to do when you're standing right in front of me!"

He chuckled and flexed his chest, the muscles popping right before her eyes. She blinked in awe, and her eyebrows shot up.

"Ogle all you want. I don't mind," he said.

So he didn't mind if she stared at him, but he obstinately turned away when he had the opportunity to stare at her? That didn't seem right, but what did she know? She blew out a breath of frustration and hurried around him, focusing on something safe. "Omelets okay for breakfast?"

"Yes, ma'am," he said.

She rushed to the kitchen section of the main area and started pulling onions, peppers, and mushrooms out of the crisper drawer of the industrial-size fridge. As she piled it all on the small island, she decided that she really liked this kitchen.

When she looked back, she startled. Isaac was watching her

just outside the bathroom, still looking glorious in nothing but his shorts.

"Oh!" she gasped. He looked so good, it took all of her self-restraint not to rush across the room and push him up against the bathroom door, kiss his neck like she had last night, taste the salt water on his skin, and then get brave and explore those lovely lips of his.

His lips turned up in a smile. With a salute, he turned and walked into the bathroom.

Cosette didn't move. She could hardly breathe. Was he just playing with her? Was he interested? What would a woman with experience do in such a situation? Was it kosher to demand to know if he was into her? Probably not. Where was Mar when she needed her?

Pulling out a cutting board, she started slicing an onion, breathing in the sharp stench. Her eyes stung, and then tears came. Pathetically, she was about ready to cry over the frustration of the entire situation, not just the onion.

CHAPTER SEVEN

The day passed slowly, and Isaac wasn't sure what to think anymore. He'd imagined yesterday that Cosette's fun-loving personality was resurfacing, and he could in good conscience tell her father that he had waited until she was healed before moving in for the long-awaited kiss. Maybe some people would claim they'd only been together for a day, but he'd been smitten with her for over a dozen years.

Yet today she'd withdrawn. He'd obviously said and done something wrong on the run and swim. When he'd tried to draw her out as they ate her delicious omelets, and he'd told her a couple of times how cute it was that she was an innocent girl and wasn't staring at or "ogling" every man's chest, she'd clammed up. Women. What man could truly understand them?

She spent most of the day either typing on her laptop or cooking. She kept a smile on her face, but he could tell she wasn't herself. Was it because of what she'd been through, or something Isaac had done? He fully appreciated the delicacies she whipped up, but when he asked if he could help, she refused, saying that she was sure he had lots he needed to be doing. Truthfully, he didn't have much to occupy himself. He tidied the small house, which was already clean except for some sand they'd tracked in; he scrubbed the bathroom, washed the dishes, sterilized the kitchen, and then shook out the rugs and swept and mopped the tile floors.

He felt like he and Cosette had taken a step back, but he wasn't sure why.

In the late afternoon, as she was working on a pasta for dinner, he went outside and raked up the fallen palm fronds, leaves, and branches from the trees and the last windstorm. It seemed impossible to imagine more than a slight breeze with the Caribbean waters so calm and the island so peaceful and beautiful, but he knew the last hurricane had wreaked intense havoc. Many parts of Puerto Rico and this island were still recovering.

Dinner was mostly quiet. Isaac complimented her on the delicious shrimp carbonara, Caesar salad, and fresh breadsticks, and he tried to draw her out with questions about her business and her friend Mar. Her answers were somewhat reserved. They'd definitely had a setback this morning. He should be relieved that he wouldn't have to fall for her and then desert her when his leave was up, but all he could think was how stupid it was to waste this time together.

He insisted on cleaning up dinner. She nodded her thanks, used the bathroom, and then wandered outside. He kept an eye on her through the window as he rushed to clean up and store the leftovers. Thankfully, she stayed pretty close, but it was getting dark out there and he didn't want her to be away from him. For security purposes and ... other reasons.

As soon as he wiped up the counter, he hurried outside, not bothering with shoes or anything else. She stopped as she heard him coming and turned to him.

"Do you want to walk?" he asked.

"Sure." She strode away from him, and he caught up. They walked a long stretch of the beach in silence and then turned and came back the other direction. It was a complete one-eighty from yesterday afternoon, when they'd sprinted the beach and laughed and talked and sprinted some more.

As they neared the house, he racked his brain for some excuse to not go to bed. He wanted her to talk to him. Before he could think of how to apologize for whatever he'd done, she said, "I'm sorry if I've been off today. I hope I haven't been … moody."

Isaac stopped, and she turned to him. "Is it because of Lansky?" he asked.

Her face showed surprise. "No, actually. I haven't been thinking of him at all."

"Oh." So there was some other reason she was off? He waited, but she didn't expound. It was like she was trying to tell him something in code.

Wait. A light bulb went on in his slow, man brain. Could it be girl stuff? His sisters were seven and nine years younger than him. He hadn't been around for Rachel's and Eve's teenage years, but he'd heard enough complaining from Seth and Caleb to know they got moody and emotional at times.

"I apologize if I did something wrong," he said, choosing his words carefully. "I don't really know to act around … girls."

Her gaze sharpened on him. Even in the deepening twilight, he could see her dark blue gaze was sharp, almost sparking. "*Girls?*"

"Well, yeah. Girls." He gestured to her. "Is there anything I can do to help?"

She folded her arms across her chest and glowered at him. "No, there's nothing you can do to help." Rolling her eyes, she muttered, "Girls. Not women, but girls?" Her voice had a definite tremble in it now.

Oh, wow. He did not want to upset her. Isaac splayed his hands, praying for diplomacy. That wasn't really his specialty, though. Give him some insurgents to hunt down any day over talking things out. "Look, I hang out with a bunch of guys all day every day. We're the furthest thing from politically correct. I'm sorry if I'm not saying this right. I would never want to offend you, and I know you've been through something hard with a man, and I know I am probably messing this all up, but—"

She held up a hand. "It's fine, Isaac. It's not your fault. Really, it isn't. But if all you see me as is a *girl* ..." She shook her head and blinked quickly. "Then there's not a lot we have to talk about anyway."

She gave him one more fake smile, then turned and pushed through the softer sand. She quickly climbed the porch steps, wiped her feet on the mat, and walked into the house. Isaac watched through the glass as she grabbed a water bottle from the fridge and then disappeared into her bedroom.

He passed a hand over his face. What had just happened? He shouldn't see her as a girl? What did she want him to see her as? She was a beautiful girl, woman, whatever, and he saw her all the time. He even saw her when he closed his eyes. Shaking his head, he wondered what to make of her obvious frustrations with him, even though she'd tried to act like all was well. She'd seen him as a man too, and he knew it. She'd stared at his chest when she'd come out of the bathroom.

Other times, he'd caught her looking at him with longing in her gaze.

Women. Girls. He definitely couldn't decipher them. Why should he even want to be with a moody, unexplainable woman anyway? He pushed out a breath. Because it was Cosette. He'd been half in love with her as a teenager. Now he was getting pushed the rest of the way. Yet she obviously wasn't returning the favor.

His phone buzzed in his pocket, and he pulled it out to read the caller ID. Blaine. Great. Not who he wanted to talk to right now.

"Jewel," Isaac said in greeting.

"Isaac," Blaine said warmly. "Everything okay there?"

Depended on your version of okay. "Quiet," he muttered. "No worries."

"How's Cosette?"

A moody beauty who was making him insane. Yet he didn't blame her; she'd been through something horrific. If only she'd let Isaac help her, hold her, love her. He shoved those unrealistic ideas away. He was her protection. Hopefully, talking to her dad would help him remember that. "She's fine. We've spent time running, swimming, and she's cooked and baked almost nonstop."

Her dad chuckled. "Sounds like her mother. Cooking always soothed both of them. I'm sure you don't mind eating it either."

"No, sir. She's an incredible cook."

"Are you ... getting too friendly?"

He wished. His mind reflected back on last night, when she'd put scents on him, leaned so close, blown on his neck, and then kissed it. They'd been friendly then. Sadly, he wasn't lying that they weren't "friendly" right now. "No, sir."

"Thank you for being there for her, son."

Isaac squinted at the quiet house. He wished he could be there for her in ways her father would not appreciate. "Of course. Any developments with Lansky?"

"I've got several private investigators following him around the clock, shooting pictures and videos. It's going great. The man's a snake and loves to intimidate, threaten, and hurt others, definitely thinks he's above the law. I think by tomorrow, or the day after, I'll have enough to turn it all over to a friend in the FBI. By the end of the week, Cosette will be safely back in her lab and you'll be heading to Florida. It'll be great."

Isaac wanted Lansky caught and punished, but he hated the thought of Cosette in her lab in San Francisco and him across the country. "Sounds great."

"I'll check back with you in a day or two."

"Thank you, sir."

"No, thank you, Isaac." Blaine's voice lowered. "I can't tell you what it means to have Cosette with someone I trust. Your family have always been there for us, and knowing that you not only have the skills but are also an honorable man means the world to me."

He wouldn't think so if he could see how Isaac had checked out his daughter today. "Thank you," Isaac said again.

"Talk to you soon." Blaine hung up.

Isaac stood on the beach for a long while. Cosette was obviously upset at him. Her father was praising him for being "honorable." If Cosette was into him, there wouldn't be much honorable about the thorough way he wanted to kiss her. Yet that wasn't fair. There was nothing wrong with kissing, and if Cosette was back to the adorable girl she'd been yesterday, he would've definitely predicted some incredible kissing tonight. As it was, he should try to rest. Who knew what tomorrow would bring with a smart, sometimes fun, always beautiful, and thoroughly confusing woman? At least there was no threat from Lansky and the security detail was a cake job. Isaac had enough on his mind trying to figure out Cosette.

Cosette rolled over in bed again. She punched her pillow, then fluffed it. She'd hardly slept last night. Why couldn't she crash tonight?

Isaac. He was in the next bedroom. Close, but so far away. Did he think she was some moody, crazy woman? No, he'd never acknowledged that she was a woman. He'd acted like she was having her time of the month and should be handled with kid gloves. Kid. Ha! There was the source of the problem. He thought of her as just a girl, and she was certain she'd played into that stereotype with her lack of social graces and her inability to look away from his bare chest. She knew she was impetuous and innocent, and okay, maybe "crazy chemist" or "Loony Lovegood" fit a little bit, but she'd thought that Isaac was drawn to her. The way he looked at her sometimes seemed to confirm it, but then he'd call her a girl, and she couldn't even count how many times he'd said she was cute, innocent, or adorable.

"Argh!" she screamed. Then she clapped a hand over her mouth.

She heard movement in the next room, and Isaac's footsteps marched across the tile floor and into the space between the rooms. He rapped softly on the door.

She lay stock-still, saying nothing. Her heart skittered out of control.

"Cosette? Cozy? You okay?" he called through the door.

"Spider!" she yelled back.

The door flung open and soft light from the mood lighting in the main area spilled in, silhouetting the delectable man, who was once again in nothing but some shorts. For the sake of Pete, he needed to put on some clothes. If he had no desire for her, she should be strong enough to stop checking him out. A shirt would help the situation immensely. Would it? His blue eyes alone made her want to beg him to hold her close.

"You okay?" Isaac asked in a rush. "Do you want me to kill it?"

"Um ... I think it's gone."

"You sure?" Isaac walked into the room, turned on the flashlight on his phone, and beamed it around.

Cosette's heart was picking up speed again. He looked so good, and he was right here. Why couldn't she kiss him and see how he responded? She wanted to prove to him that she was a woman, not a little girl. Yet what if her kissing skills stank as bad as Vance claimed? The thought kept her frozen to the bed.

"I don't see anything," Isaac finally said. He shut off the light and turned to her with a smile creasing his handsome face. "Hopefully you can sleep now."

"Thanks. I'm sure I will." She faked a brave smile and pressed her arms along her sides on top of the thin sheet covering her.

His gaze roved over her form in the bed, and his smile disappeared. "Good night," he said quickly before hurrying out of the room and shutting the door behind him.

Cosette lay there, almost panting for air from the way he'd

looked at her. That had been the gaze of a man looking at a woman. Was there hope?

Rolling over, she realized that she had hardly thought about Vance since coming here. Isaac filled up all her brain space. If only she had a chance with him. The terror and belittlement of Vance would definitely be a distant memory.

CHAPTER EIGHT

Isaac finally fell asleep, thinking about Cosette far too late into the night. How could he get to the bottom of what she was feeling? How could he restore her innocent happiness and in good conscience pursue her?

He woke late with the sun already streaming into the large windows. Hurrying, he dressed in workout clothes and brushed his teeth. He scrubbed at the days' growth on his cheeks. Did Cosette like him clean shaven? Did she like him at all?

Walking out into the main room, he found Cosette already there. She was wearing a fitted tank top and shorts, and she bent forward, hugging her arms and swaying side to side. "Morning," she said from her upside-down perch.

"Morning." He tried to pull his gaze away, but he couldn't.

She straightened and gave him an embarrassed smile. "Ogling," she said in a semi-teasing tone.

Isaac laughed and passed a hand over his face. "Definitely."

She seemed more herself this morning. Was the moodiness

of yesterday gone? Was that how it worked for girls? What man knew? Not him.

"Ready to run?" she asked.

"Sure." Isaac grabbed a water bottle and chugged it down before following her outside. They ran the opposite direction of yesterday and found more stretches of beautiful beach. They didn't talk much, and Cosette seemed to be pushing herself harder today, keeping up a faster pace. Isaac wouldn't have minded going slower and being able to chat, but he followed her lead.

As they arrived back at the house, she glanced at him, pulling in quick breaths. "Swimming again?"

"Sure." Swimming sounded great, and he wasn't about to miss out on an opportunity to be with her. He tugged off his sweaty shirt and dropped it.

Cosette was studying him openly, which he found encouraging. They both removed their shoes and socks and waded into the water. Swimming out a little ways in the softly rolling ocean, they stopped and treaded water. Isaac hoped this was his moment. He prayed he'd say *something* right. There was nothing for it but to open his big, fat mouth and try. He couldn't make it any worse. Well, there were no promises of that.

"Hey." He swallowed hard and rushed out, "I'm sorry about yesterday. I'm afraid I offended you with the comments about women. Like I said, I don't have much experience with girls in my special ops unit, and my sisters are a lot younger than me." He was rambling with excuses and didn't know if it was helping or not.

"Women?" Her gaze was sharp on him. He loved those deep blue eyes of hers, but he felt a sense of trepidation; she was already acting like he was doing something wrong. It was worse than wading through a field planted with IEDs. "Or *girls?*"

He pushed at the water with his hands, shrugging. "What's the difference?"

Her eyes narrowed then. "What do you mean, what's the difference?" She pushed out a huffy breath and splashed some water in his face.

Isaac wiped it away, wishing he could grab her firm body and dunk her under the water, but she wasn't being playful, more frustrated. He asked carefully, "Please help me out here, Cozy. What did I do wrong now?"

"You're doing everything wrong," she shot at him.

Isaac had to somehow figure this out. "I'm sorry," he said. "Men are not built to understand women. I don't know why that is, but I'm coming to realize it's all too true."

Cosette shook her head. "I don't care if you understand women, Isaac, and I'm honestly glad you don't have a lot of experience figuring my gender out." Her gaze was fiery and impertinent. "Do you think of me as a woman or as a child?"

"What?" Isaac was confused now. "Cosette, you're the most beautiful woman I've ever encountered. How could you think for a second that I view you as a child?" That was disgusting and wrong.

She stared at him, tilting her head to the side and wrinkling her brow in puzzlement. "You're being serious right now, aren't you?"

"Dead serious," he shot back. "You are all woman to me."

Her cheeks flushed, but she was still looking at him as if he were from a different planet. "You've called me a girl, adorable, innocent, and cute. You've never once said I was a woman, let alone a beautiful woman ... until now." But her eyes had softened at his last line, and he thought they were finally getting somewhere.

Isaac passed a hand over his face, wetting it. He wrapped one arm around her waist, loving her little squeak of surprise and the warmth of her body against his, and then he swam for the shore. When the water was waist deep, he forced himself to release her. "Cosette, when I say you're adorable, innocent, or cute, it doesn't mean I think of you as a child. It means I think you're refreshing, amazing, unique."

She blinked up at him and bit at her lip. He wanted to kiss her, but he wasn't sure that they were there yet. Tonight? He could hope.

"You're an accomplished, brilliant, and beautiful woman," he said carefully so she knew he was sincere. "I am extremely impressed with you and wouldn't offend you for the world."

Cosette's face lit up with a beautiful smile. She launched herself against him, gave him a tight hug, and then pulled back too quickly for him to savor the feeling of having her close.

"Thank you!" she said. "Oh!" She raised her shoulders in the cutest gesture—or the most attractive gesture, he should say. "You've made me so happy. I'm going to cook now. Well, after I shower." She squeezed his arm. "Waffles?"

Isaac nodded dumbly, his head still spinning at this one-eighty. He'd made her upset by using the word girl instead of woman. Now she was restored. He wasn't about to complain, but he still didn't see how she could ever think he viewed her as a child, and he'd honestly rather sit and hold her and talk to her than have her cook for him again. But he wasn't dumb enough to voice any objections right now.

She gave him one more happy smile, then turned and pushed through the water. He didn't turn away this time. When she bent down to scoop up her shoes, he pulled in a loud breath. Cosette glanced over her shoulder at him and gave him a broad wink. His heart was hammering, threatening to burst out of his chest. She walked slowly up to the house, swinging her hips in such an appealing way, it was all he could do to not push through the water, sprint at her, and tackle her into the sand.

She stopped on the top step and checked to see if he was still looking. When she saw that he was, she beamed and called to him, "You're ogling your woman, Captain Jewel."

Isaac chuckled. He saluted her. She gave him a sassy flip of her long hair and strode into the house. He watched through the glass until she disappeared in the bathroom, and then he lay back and floated in the water, staring up at the blue sky. Everything had changed. Excitement rushed through him. Were there still reasons he needed to be cautious and not just kiss her until they both had to come up for air? If there were, he couldn't think of them.

Your woman. She'd said that, called herself *his* woman. His heart beat out of rhythm just thinking about it. Yet she'd also reminded him that he was Captain Jewel. He was going back. If she truly became his and he kissed her and fell for her like he yearned to do, how would he leave her?

―――

Cosette rushed through her shower in a happy daze. Isaac didn't think she was a little girl; he thought she was a beautiful, accomplished, and brilliant woman. Ooh, she wanted to squeal. Today was the best day of her entire life. Could he truly like her the way she liked him? Had she really called herself his woman? Was that too presumptuous? Would he kiss her? Her stomach filled up with butterflies at the very idea, and she shoved away Vance's snide comments about her kissing abilities.

Brushing out her hair and putting on some makeup, she dressed in a floral sundress and hurried to start the waffles. It was quiet except for the birds twittering outside and the tide softly rolling in. She wondered where Isaac was, and she cast her gaze outside and spotted him out floating in the sea. He came in while she was separating egg yolks and whites. Her hands were shaky as she accidentally dropped a bit of shell into the yolks.

"Hey," he said, his face splitting in a grin as his eyes swept over her. "You look beautiful."

"I, um …" Her hands were full of eggshells, and her heart was full of his look and compliment. He looked amazing, with his dark hair pushed back from his handsome face, his tanned, muscular chest glistening with water droplets, and—most importantly—his blue eyes focused on her. "Do you want chocolate chips or blueberries in your waffles?"

His eyebrows shot up. Probably not the response he was planning on. "Chocolate chips are an option?"

"Of course."

"Definitely chocolate chips."

She smiled. He was perfect for her. She'd always choose chocolate over fruit.

He held his shirt up, and the muscles in his arm flexed smoothly in response. "I'll just go shower," he said.

"What do you do to have muscles like that?" she demanded before he could walk away.

Isaac's smile grew and his blue eyes twinkled. "I'm naturally built this way."

She dropped the shell in the garbage, rinsed off her hands, and wagged a finger at him. "Don't give me that nonsense."

He chuckled. "We have a pretty strict regimen of healthy eating and exercise with my unit." He pumped his eyebrows at her and said, "Are you getting more comfortable seeing my bare chest, then?"

Her face flared red, but she forced herself to stare steadily at him. "Ogling it, you mean?"

His laughter increased. He folded his arms across his chest. "Yes, ogling," he said.

"It's not any trouble for me to look at it," she said.

His smile grew. "Well, I'm glad to hear that." He winked and then strode into the bathroom.

It was rough to focus on a perfect consistency for waffles when she heard the shower running, and especially when Isaac walked from the bathroom to his bedroom in only a towel—he muttered, "Sorry, forgot my clothes," but his unapologetic look said that he knew exactly how he affected her. She had an entire stack of waffles ready when he came out of his bedroom with his dark hair swept back, looking fresh and perfect in a white T-shirt and navy-blue shorts.

"It smells good," he said.

"Thank you."

She said a prayer, and they ate, talking about what they were going to do today. Isaac thought they could go explore the island a little bit. There were no indicators that Vance was coming after her, and he shared that her dad had investigators taking pictures and videos and thought it would all be over soon.

She definitely wanted Vance arrested, but she didn't want to cut short her time with Isaac. They were just getting comfortable with each other, and there was a myriad of things she wanted to experience with him, first of all a lovely kiss. She was still afraid of being horrible at kissing like Vance had told her, but she wasn't going to let that jerk keep her from trying.

They finished eating and worked together to clean up. Cosette turned from the island counter with a handful of dishes and bumped into Isaac, who smiled down at her. She wished her hands were free so she could wrap her arms around him and hold on.

He leaned down and brushed the hair over her shoulder. "I love this dress on you," he murmured.

Cosette took a deep breath, and her smile grew. "You're wearing it."

"The cologne you gave me?" At her nod, he said, "Of course I'm wearing it. I want to smell ... irresistible to you."

Cosette set the dishes in the sink, wiped her hands dry, and admitted, "You are irresistible to me in every which way."

Isaac grinned.

"I really appreciate you wearing the cologne," she said. "Vance wouldn't wear my cologne, said it was 'box store' cologne." She tossed her hair, angry at the memory for surfacing when she might have been having a moment with Isaac. She was inexperienced, but she wasn't stupid. Well, maybe she was stupid. She'd just brought up Vance.

Isaac's grin fled. "Cozy," he murmured. "We need to talk about some ... stuff."

Cosette didn't like the sound of that, but when he took her hand and led her to the couch, she sat down close beside him. The perfect smell of the cologne she'd created mingled with his body chemistry, flooding her with good feelings that repelled Vance's belittlement. "What do we need to talk about?" she asked.

"Vance."

She blew out a breath. Maybe she couldn't push Vance away just yet. "Why would we want to talk about him?"

His blue eyes were somber as they met hers. "I love seeing your happy personality restored. At the risk of getting hit, you are ... adorable."

She smacked his arm, mostly because he'd said she'd hit him, but she knew what he meant. "I want to be my happy, carefree self again too. Aside from getting frustrated with you yesterday, I've felt more like myself with you here than I have in a while."

He nodded. "I'm glad. I've watched some friends and teammates go through horrible stuff. I'm no psychotherapist, but sometimes I was all they had, as I'm their captain and one of the few who believes in God. Most of the time I would pray with them and then just let them talk. Some still needed medication and therapy when we got back to base, but for some it was enough."

"You're so impressive," she said. "I love that you could help them, and that you're strong enough to be a man of faith and not be embarrassed about it or hide it."

"Thank you." He paused and studied her. "Do you want to pray and talk about what happened with Vance?"

Cosette's eyes widened. She'd been too slow to figure out what Isaac was trying to do. She couldn't tell him about how Vance had romanced her up until a few weeks ago, when he'd brought her to Vegas and started a campaign of belittlement. She and Isaac had just started to connect, to hopefully become a couple like she'd always dreamed of. Telling him all the things Vance had found wrong with her would paint her in a horrible light and probably make Isaac question why he'd want to be with her. Vance was a low-life jerk, but there was a grain of truth in all he'd seen wrong with her. She was flighty, unpredictable, awful in social situations, inexperienced at kissing ... On and on the list went. "Um ... no."

"No?" Isaac looked stunned; this was obviously not the answer he'd been hoping for.

"I'm fine, but thank you so much for offering. I'll remember this if I ever need to talk things out." Cosette stood and swept the wrinkles out of her dress with her palms. "So how are we going to tour the island if we have no car?"

Isaac stood too. His blue eyes filled with concern, and his mouth pursed. "You're sure you don't want to talk?"

"Very sure. Thank you so much. Are we walking, then? Running shoes might look a little funny with this dress, but that's all right." She gave him what she hoped was a blinding smile, certain that her responses weren't right, but she didn't care. She was not talking to him about Vance.

Isaac swallowed, passed a hand over his jaw, and then said, "I found a golf cart in the shed." He tilted his head outside. "Should be a fun way to explore."

She clapped her hands together. "That's perfect. Can I drive?"

He finally cracked a smile. "Why do I have the feeling I'm taking my life into my hands?"

"'Cause you're a wuss." She laughed at calling this ultra-tough special ops hero a wuss. "I'm an amazing driver. Especially in a golf cart. My parents loved to golf, but I stank at it. Too much patience for no reward. So they'd let me drive the cart around." She wrinkled her nose at him. She hoped he'd think she was being her happy, "adorable" self and wouldn't pursue the line of questioning about Vance again. "Let's go!"

She hurried for her bedroom and grabbed some lip gloss, a hat, and her sandals. Her hands were shaking slightly. She clasped her hat between them and bowed her head. *Please help Isaac to fall for me and not ask questions about Vance*, she begged. Then she squared her shoulders and hurried out to spend the day with Isaac. Nothing could have made her happier. If only there wasn't the black cloud of Vance hanging over their heads.

CHAPTER NINE

As they traversed the island of Vieques, Isaac tried to push away his concerns over what Lansky might have done to Cosette. The island was over twenty miles long east to west, but only about four miles north to south. They checked out the town of Isabella nearby before cruising south in the golf cart, stopping first at El Fortín Conde de Mirasol Museum and touring it.

After they finished at the fort, they tried out Mama Mia's Pizza. Isaac thought it was fabulous, but Cosette claimed she was still stuffed from breakfast and only managed to polish off one piece. Getting back in the golf cart, she declared she was driving again. The thing probably topped out at twenty-five miles per hour, but as she drove, she grinned like she was on an amusement ride.

They headed south and then east, driving through part of the wildlife reserve. They made a stop at Secret Beach and walked and waded in the water for a little bit. Cosette was cussing herself for not bringing a swimsuit. She teased Isaac that he didn't need one; he could just strip his shirt off.

Cosette acted as fun and innocent as he'd remembered her as a teenager. She was impulsive—and yes, adorable—as she talked with locals and tourists alike, exploring and taking in the island sites with childlike innocence, and yet she was definitely all woman. It still confused him that she would think he didn't know she was a grown woman. He knew she was, and he noticed far too often. Could he pursue a relationship with her while knowing she was damaged from something Lansky had done?

They finally arrived at Esperanza on the south side of the island with its beautiful bay and old pier stretching out into the crystal-blue water. They ate sandwiches at a local shop, talking the entire time with the owner, who was about their age. He'd lived in the States until he'd graduated high school; then he'd started wandering through the Caribbean islands. When he'd landed on Vieques, he'd started his shop and never looked back.

The guy flirted with Cosette, and she teased and laughed with him. Isaac knew it meant nothing, but he felt a stir of jealousy anyway. And that brought him back around to Lansky. Why wouldn't Cosette talk to him about their relationship? Maybe it was none of his business. He and Cosette weren't an official couple—they hadn't even kissed—but he wanted to protect her and love her.

The sandwich shop guy told Cosette all about the great snorkeling right off the old Sugar Cane Pier, regaling her with stories of seeing eels, rays, turtles, all manner of fish, and even a shark.

"Can we snorkel?" Cosette begged him.

"Sure." Isaac shrugged. "Do you want to go back and get suits or ... Can we buy her a swimsuit close by?"

"Of course," the sandwich guy said, pointing. "Shop right

there." He winked. "Perfect suits for the beautiful lady, and they have snorkel gear too."

Isaac thanked him and tugged Cosette away. They got outfitted with new swimsuits, towels, and some cheap snorkel masks and tried out the snorkeling by the pier. They did see a lot of colorful fish around the algae-covered pylons, and Isaac liked holding Cosette's hand and swimming languidly around while they studied the underwater world.

The sun was dipping toward the west as they dried off next to the pier. Cosette slipped her dress over her head, and Isaac put his shirt back on. A band was playing next to some of the outdoor restaurants by the pier. Cosette's eyes lit up at the sound of the music. "Let's dance."

He couldn't resist her. "Sure."

They dropped their snorkeling gear and extra clothes into the back of the golf cart and headed to the small square, where the band was playing some upbeat Latin music and a few couples were dancing.

"Do you like to dance?" Isaac asked.

"Like it?" Cosette's navy-blue eyes sparkled. "I love it." She started to demonstrate. It was all Isaac could do to hide a laugh as she danced. She flailed around, she gyrated, she twirled her hips one way and her arms another, she threw her hair back and forth, and then she imitated a native belly dancing of sorts. It was the cutest thing he'd ever seen, and she was possibly the worst dancer he'd ever encountered—maybe because most people that danced this horribly would never do it in public.

Isaac tried to dance next to her as people were starting to stare, but finally he couldn't take it anymore. He wrapped his arms around her and tucked her in close to his body. "C'mere," he murmured. "Let's dance together."

She smiled up at him so sweetly, catching her breath from her dancing, if it could be called that. He found himself breathing more quickly as well as he held her tight in his arms. Luckily, the song changed to a slow beat at the same time. It might not have been luck; even the band had been watching Cosette's crazy display and exchanging looks with raised eyebrows.

Cosette wrapped her arms around his lower back and laid her head on his chest. Even slow dancing, she couldn't seem to find the beat, never swaying with the rhythm of the song. Isaac didn't care, though; he vowed that if they ever got married, there would be no dancing at their wedding.

That thought startled him. He couldn't get married. Sure, there were some men in his troop who were married, but it was a risky thing to go under fire and into dangerous situations like they did and leave a wife and possibly children behind. It was hard enough leaving his parents and siblings.

He pushed that aside and concentrated on the perfect way Cosette fit in his arms. Bending down close, he said, "We probably should get back. I don't think the golf cart has lights."

"Oh! Yeah, we'd better go."

Isaac took her hand and led her to the golf cart. "Do you want to drive?"

"No, you can."

He climbed in, and she snuggled close to his side. Isaac didn't mind that at all. He pushed the golf cart to the max speed, but he still didn't think they hit thirty miles per hour. The sun set, and their light was fading fast. They'd made the turn to head east to their house and he knew they were getting close, but complete darkness fell around them. He pulled out his phone flashlight, and Cosette held it out to light the way while they puttered down the road and eventually made it back to the house.

Once he'd parked the golf cart in the shed, they walked into the house hand in hand. Isaac thought they should definitely spend some time snuggling on the couch, talking, kissing, and seeing what happened.

Cosette smiled at him, went on tiptoes, and kissed his cheek. "Thank you. Today was perfect."

"Thank you," he said.

She grinned and then traipsed into the bathroom. He heard the shower start and thought it might be time for him to check the security cameras outside. This woman was exactly what he wanted, but he still hadn't come to terms with loving her and leaving her. Truthfully, she was driving him insane.

Cosette came out of the bathroom after her shower only to find that Isaac wasn't in the main area. A quick dart of disappointment went through her. She'd daydreamed throughout her shower about dancing all alone in the dark. In her imagination, that led to kissing. She rubbed her hands together in anticipation. She smiled, thinking back on their day. She'd loved every minute with him. He treated her like an angel and was so much fun to be with. A frown pulled her lips down as she realized they only had four days left before Isaac would have to go back to Florida. Hopefully Vance would be arrested by then, but she was more concerned about more time with Isaac.

She went into her room, put on a tank top and some shorts, and lay down on the bed. She left the door open, hoping she'd hear Isaac or he'd come in to say good night. Kissing her good night would be even better. Closing her eyes, she listened to the ocean softly rolling onto the beach. A mental image of Isaac grinned at her with a sparkle in his blue eyes.

The next thing she knew, she startled awake. The house was dark, except for the mood lights in the main area, and quiet. Only the sound of the tide broke the silence. She'd fallen asleep and missed the chance to kiss Isaac after their wonderful day together. No!

Scrambling out of bed, she darted out of her room and flung Isaac's door open wide. "Isaac," she called to him.

"What?" He sprang up in bed, quickly pushing to his feet. "Are you okay? What's wrong?"

Cosette strode up to him and threw her arms around his strong back. "I forgot to give you something today."

"What?" He was still looking a little disoriented. His blue eyes stared at her in confusion, his hair was mussed, and his beautiful chest was visible.

"This." She arched up and pressed her lips to his.

Isaac startled and pulled slightly away from her. Every fear that she was a horrible kisser like Vance had claimed came rushing back. That kiss was too short to really know, though. Would Isaac give her another chance? Would he teach her to be better? He was taken with her, and she wanted him.

"You needed to give me that?" Isaac asked in a gravelly voice. He tenderly cupped her face with his hands and stared down at her.

"Yes, I did." Cosette wrapped her hands around his biceps and pulled herself tighter to him, praying he wouldn't push her away.

"Thank you," Isaac murmured. Then he dipped his head and he kissed her. Wow, did he kiss her.

The darkness around them seemed to sparkle, but that might have just been how lit up Cosette felt from the inside out. Isaac's mouth took command of hers, and everything from his warm, strong body to his delectable cologne made the kiss absolutely perfect. It was better than dancing, better than cooking, better than working in her lab, better than anything her overactive imagination could dream up, and that was saying something.

Isaac continued to kiss her but put his hands on her hips and easily lifted her off the ground. Cosette wrapped her legs around his waist and leaned down to him, hungrily returning his kisses and not wanting to be pulled apart for one second.

He carried her out to the couch, sinking down with her now sitting on his lap. Isaac pulled back slightly and said with a smile, "It's a better idea to not be kissing you in my bedroom."

"Oh?" she asked, a little bit confused. Then images of what might happen if they kept kissing in the bedroom raced through her, and with those ideas came a heat that threatened to blister. "Oh!" She scrambled off of his lap and onto her own couch cushion. "I didn't mean to ... Oh my!"

Isaac chuckled, wrapped an arm around her, and pulled her in close to his side. "I know you didn't. You're so innocent and perfect."

Cosette glanced up at him. "Are you sure those two coincide?" she asked quietly.

"Yes." He nodded firmly, lifting her sideways onto his lap and against his chest. "Innocent, perfect, beautiful, irresistible, adorable ... You're the perfect combination of all things good and desirable, Cozy. You're perfect to me."

Cosette sighed happily and had no choice but to kiss him again. Granted, it wasn't any hardship on her part. The kisses grew in intensity and passion, and she knew she'd never been kissed like this before. He was hers. She felt it. She'd spent most of her life in her own head, imagining and creating and experimenting. She couldn't create something as beautiful as the connection between them, but she could spend a long time experimenting with different ways to kiss him.

When he gently deepened the kiss and tingles went off everywhere in her mouth, she cried out, "Oh!" and pulled back, staring at him in shock and awe. "That was ..."

"Too quick," Isaac said. "I'm sorry."

"Don't you ever be sorry about kissing me," she said fiercely. "Let's try it again, without me freaking out."

He chuckled and moved in close. "Yes, ma'am."

Time passed in this perfect activity, and Cosette was invigorated yet content from all the kissing and the knowledge that she'd finally found the man she was destined to be with. Her imagination ran wild with a white dress and a tux at a beach wedding, then a little bungalow like this for just the two of them, until a whole bundle of kiddos came to challenge and increase their blessed happiness.

She pulled back from a lingering kiss and murmured, "I want to be with you forever, Isaac."

His eyes went from half closed and full of desire to wide open and full of concern. He ushered her next to him on the couch and held her against him with one arm. Cosette curled into him, resting her hand on his chest. Had she said something wrong?

"Cozy," he murmured, placing a soft kiss on her forehead. "I have to go back to Florida in four days."

Her body tightened with worry. "I know that. I'm not asking you to give up your career for me."

Isaac nodded, his chin brushing her hair. "I know you

wouldn't, but I don't see how we can make something long-term work. I don't have any plans to retire from the military or take a desk job anytime soon, and I would never ask you to give up your lab and business in San Fran to follow me around the world from base to base."

Cosette sat there, slowly coming back down to reality. All the joy and sparkles of their kissing session faded like a burnt-out firework as she realized he had no intention of even trying to make this work in the long run. She was the one who had come on to him and kissed him. She was the one who'd impetuously claimed that she wanted to be with him forever, with unrealistic dreams to boot.

Her inexperience with men and relationships was rearing its ugly head again. Isaac had obviously enjoyed kissing her, and he'd been honorable about not doing it in the bedroom and risking anything untoward happening. He was a good man, one of the best, but it was painfully obvious that he couldn't feel everything she felt if he could let ugly reality expose the impracticality of a future relationship. She wouldn't even have brought up reality. She preferred to make promises, live in the clouds, and when they had to separate, they would deal with it somehow.

Standing, she forced a smile. "We'd better get some sleep." She started toward her bedroom.

Isaac sprang up and followed her. Wrapping his hands around her waist, he pulled her back against his solid chest and held her there. After a few wonderful moments in his arms, she didn't know how she'd resist him. They could kiss until he had to return to base. She wouldn't say stupid things about forever. It wasn't in her nature to worry anyway. But a future without Isaac? That sounded awful.

"I'm sorry, Cozy," he whispered against her cheek. "I'm sorry that I don't know how to make us work."

Pain ripped through her. "It'll be fine," she lied through clenched teeth. "It'll all work out. Good night." Yanking free of his grip, she hurried into her bedroom and shut the door tight. She tried to keep her mind focused on their beautiful kissing session and all the compliments Isaac had given her, not the way the night had ended and his inability to even try to have a future.

When she realized that tears were sliding silently down her face, she gave up focusing on the positive and let herself have a good cry.

CHAPTER TEN

Isaac finally crashed early the next morning; he'd stayed up and berated himself for being a practical idiot instead of just enjoying every second of Cosette in his arms. He didn't know how to change what he'd said, though, because it was true. They were both highly invested in their careers, and he couldn't see either of them making a change. Long-distance relationships had never worked for him in the past. He'd give it his all for Cosette, but he wondered if it would be enough for either of them. He didn't want some halfway relationship with her. Her kisses had filled him with joy and light. He wanted to be close to her every minute he could, to protect and love her.

Groaning, he pushed out of bed when the sun was far higher in the sky than it should have been. Cosette was waiting for him in the main area. She was wearing a bright smile and her running clothes, sitting on the couch with a novel that she'd probably found on the shelves next to all the DVDs. "I've been waiting for you all morning," she said, all chipper and cute.

"Sorry," Isaac said, not even sure what he was apologizing for: sleeping in, or kissing her like it was his last night on earth and then telling her he was still going to ditch her.

"No worries." Her smile didn't falter, but her eyes were darker than normal and red rimmed. Had she been crying? No. He'd take basic training again over knowing he'd made Cosette cry.

He drank some water and tied his shoes, and then they walked out of the house and set off down the beach. It was hot, and he was tired and miserable. When they finally turned around, he was relieved.

As they got back to the house, swimming in the ocean looked like the perfect thing to do, but Cosette said, "What do you say we actually put suits on and try out the snorkel gear here?"

"Sure."

They changed into their suits and snorkeled for a while but didn't find much.

As they both swam back to the beach, giving up on seeing anything besides sand and the occasional seashell through the crystal-clear water, Cosette asked, "Is there another good place to snorkel around here?"

"Let me find out." He got his phone and Googled "best snorkeling on the north side of Vieques." "Mosquito Pier isn't too far, just past the airport," he told her.

"Great. Let's do it." She was so bright and happy. Isaac wanted to be happy with her, but that would be difficult with everything lingering between them.

They ate a simple breakfast of oatmeal, packed up snacks, drinks, and towels, and took the golf cart to Mosquito Bay, where they found the pier and had a good snorkel. They saw lots of fish, some sea turtles, and even some of the rays they'd been promised to see at the other side of the island.

They ate at a Crabwalk Café on the way back to the house, talking about superficial things. Cosette never fully met his gaze, but she always acted perky and cute.

Isaac had messed up. He knew that. If only he knew how to fix it.

When they got back to the house, they each showered and Cosette got started on cooking. Isaac offered to help, but she winked and said that she was the chef and he shouldn't worry. He walked outside, basically circling the house over and over again, wondering what to do with himself and how to make things right with Cosette. *Not worry?* Yeah, right.

His phone rang. He pulled it out with a scowl, but he relaxed a little bit when he saw it was Luke instead of Blaine. Come to think of it, it was odd that he hadn't heard from Blaine. He'd call tonight if he didn't hear something soon.

"Hey, bro," Luke said. "How's the vacation?"

Isaac smiled. "Vieques is beautiful."

"Is Cosette beautiful?"

"You know she is." He passed his free hand over his face.

"You two having fun together?"

"I think I'm falling for her."

Luke pulled in a loud breath. "Well, all right, then. Perfect. You two settle down in San Fran near her dad and her lab, make beautiful, spacey children. It's perfect."

Isaac was back to scowling again. "I'm not leaving the Air Force."

"Oh. That does make it more difficult."

"Yeah. Did you call for a reason?" He continued his pacing

around the house and the beach, never straying too far from Cosette. She was still right there in the kitchen, cooking away.

"Not really, just to razz you."

Isaac shook his head. "What are you working on now?"

"Buying up property to build hundreds and hundreds of storage units. Do you realize how much crap Americans have and how unwilling they are to part with it? It's a gold mine, bro."

"Good for you."

They talked for a few more minutes before saying goodbye. Isaac put his phone in his pocket and studied Cosette through the glass. She caught him looking and flashed him a smile before turning away. He'd told his brother that he was falling for her, but that was a lie. He was far past that. He loved her. Shaking his head, he resumed his pacing.

Cosette thought she'd put on a pretty good face today. She'd enjoyed being around Isaac, snorkeling, and cooking. She wasn't worried about Vance at all, but she was worried about Isaac. There was a tightness around his eyes and mouth that revealed his concern. He cared for her, but he didn't know how they could make a future work. She'd never felt more grounded in reality, and she'd never wanted to be in her happy headspace more. Reality stank.

They cleaned up the orange chicken, veggies, and fried rice. The sun had barely set; it wasn't even full dark outside. Glancing nervously around, she had no clue what to do with the time. She was wishing time away, yet at the same time she wanted to savor each minute with Isaac.

He seemed to be a little unsure as well. It was an endearing, disconcerting look on this tough, confident man.

"Walk on the beach?" she asked.

"Sure." He gave her a fake smile and a nod.

They walked outside together and along the beach. It was perfect, quiet, and romantic. If only Isaac would take her hand. Their arms brushed, and warmth started in the pit of her stomach. They might not be able to carve out a future, but why were they missing these moments? She grabbed his hand in hers and held on tight.

Isaac's gaze darted to her. She smiled brightly at him and squeezed his hand. At least he didn't pull away. "You know what I think?" she asked.

"No, what's that?"

She was scared, terrified. The next words would be worse than jumping off a cliff, or so she figured. She'd never actually jumped off a cliff. Maybe she should try it, if she could hold Isaac's hand while doing so.

When she didn't say anything, Isaac prompted, "Cozy?"

"We're being stupid," she pushed out.

Isaac stopped walking and turned to her, clinging to her hand. "Wanting a future together is stupid?"

So he did want a future together? That was good news. All he'd really said last night was that they couldn't have a future together. "*That* isn't stupid, but we don't have all the answers about it right now. So what? Why are we wasting this time we have together?" She raised an eyebrow and put her other hand on her hip, tossing her long hair. "Hmm?"

Isaac smiled and shook his head. "You are entirely too appealing." He released her hand, wrapped his arms around her lower back, and pulled her tight against him.

Cosette let out a little squeal of surprise, which made him

smile bigger. She slid her hands up his broad shoulders and around his upper back.

Isaac's smile fled, and his blue eyes filled with longing for her. "So what do you suggest, my beautiful scientist? Do you have a theory for how to make us work?"

Cosette stared up at him, lost in his gaze. "I think all we can do is enjoy the moments, take it a day at a time."

"That seems shortsighted."

She frowned at him. "It might be, but it's all we have right now. I'll take whatever I can get with you."

"Ooh, that's a little forward," he teased.

Cosette rolled her eyes. "You know what I mean." She tightened her grip on him and pulled herself up closer to his lips. "Let's savor this, savor us. If the future is hard and lonely, at least we'll have this time."

Isaac didn't look like he loved it, but he rubbed his palms over her lower back and made her body warm up. "So what exactly did you want to savor?" he asked.

Cosette smiled and bit at her lip. Bending toward his neck, she breathed him in. His delicious scent made her a little weak in the knees.

"Are you sniffing me?" he asked.

"Yes, sir ... and you're completely irresistible."

He smiled.

Cosette softly kissed his neck. As she coyly looked up at him to check his reaction, she blew warm air on his neck like she had two nights ago when they'd been trying out colognes.

Isaac pulled in a sharp breath, bent his head to hers, and captured her mouth with his own. Light and joy filled her as they kissed without restraint. Isaac's lips took command of her every thought, and there were no worries about the future with him.

Of course they'd be together. Something this wonderful didn't come along every day. What kind of idiots would they be to not make it work?

Isaac slowed the kisses down and then ushered her head to his chest and held her close.

"Can we make it work?" she asked, not looking up. If he wanted to reject her, it would be easier without her staring at him.

Isaac released one hand from her back and tilted her chin up. His palm cupped her cheek, and he tenderly drew his thumb across her bottom lip. Cosette trembled from his touch.

"We'll make it work," he promised.

"I love you." She gasped, realizing that it was probably far too early for such talk.

Isaac didn't look shocked or like she was crazy, too impulsive, or out of line. He gave her a tender kiss and whispered against her lips, "I love you too."

Cosette gave a happy cry and then kissed him fiercely. He chuckled against her mouth and returned each kiss with passion and love that she knew wouldn't dim. So a long-distance relationship would be awful. It didn't matter. They'd have time together when he was on leave, and they'd savor it.

She felt a weird buzzing against Isaac's hip. Ignoring it, she kept kissing him. But the buzzing was insistent.

"I'd better get that," he said.

Cosette bit back the disappointment and eased back enough for him to pull his phone out.

"Jewel," he answered sharply. His gaze stayed focused on her, but that gaze went from tender to concerned to horrified. "Excuse me?" he said. "Who are you again?" A pause. "I understand. We'll be there as soon as possible."

Cosette felt the fear of whatever was coming before Isaac ended the call. He kept one arm around her, the other clutching his phone.

"Cozy." His voice was reluctant, worried. "Lansky has your dad."

Cosette's legs wouldn't support her. Isaac held her against his side. He quickly dropped his phone in his pocket and swooped her up into his arms, cradling her close.

She let out a cry. Vance had her dad. How could this be happening? Bile rose in her throat as she imagined her dad being held down by those brutes while Vance carved up his back. "No!" she screamed. "No!"

"It'll be okay," Isaac tried to reassure her, but she could hear the emptiness of his reassurance. "That was the FBI. One of his private investigators noticed he hadn't been checking in, and when he couldn't get a response via email, text, or phone, he went to search your dad's house. There was a note left on the counter with instructions for when and where you should meet Vance to get your dad back. The FBI's involved. I'll be right with you. It'll all be okay."

Cosette appreciated his levelheadedness and calm, but she'd never been either and she wasn't about to start now. "He's all I have left," she groaned.

A fierce light came into Isaac's eyes. "No," he corrected. "You have me too. And I promise you I'll rescue your dad and Lansky will pay. I promise you."

Cosette nodded at him, then cuddled against his chest. Lansky could be torturing her dad even now. The thought made a sob rip from her throat. She screwed her eyes tight and said a fierce prayer. Her faith and Isaac's strength were the only things she could rely on right now.

CHAPTER ELEVEN

Isaac got ahold of Joshua, and thankfully Joshua was still at the Jewel Resort on the main island of Puerto Rico. His brother's plane was waiting for them at the tiny Vieques airport within the hour. They boarded Joshua's luxurious jet, and Isaac hoped Cosette would relax now that they were moving the right direction, but it was obvious that she couldn't calm down. Somehow, that loser Lansky had turned this around on them and captured Blaine. That was bad enough, but more concerning was the fact that Lansky hadn't asked for any ransom or negotiation. He'd simply demanded that Cosette meet him tomorrow night at ten on the San Francisco Piers.

It was after ten when they departed Vieques. Isaac and Cosette were in full-on recliners, but she clutched his hand so desperately that he didn't know that she'd relax enough in the next eight hours to get any sleep. They both needed sleep.

He excused himself to look through Joshua's bathroom cupboards. Luckily, there was a bottle of ZzzQuil natural sleep aids. He brought the box back to Cosette. She peered up at him with red eyes in the darkened interior of the plane. His heart swelled within him. This woman loved him. He'd do anything to protect her.

Sitting down next to her, he lied, "Cozy, I really need to sleep so I'll be as sharp as possible when we meet with Lansky tomorrow night. Will you please take these with me?"

She squinted at the box. "It's all natural?"

"That's what it says." He tried to smile reassuringly. He would be fine without sleep. He'd done it many times in his career and still performed with exactness. She was the one he was worried about. He opened the package and took four gummies out, placing two in her palm. "You go first."

She shook her head. "Together."

"Okay." Isaac put the gummies in his mouth and chewed, relieved when she did the same. She weighed half what he or Joshua did, and if Joshua had these things in his plane and they were effective for his large frame, they should knock Cosette out completely.

They each took a drink of water to get the gummy bear taste out of their mouths. Isaac pushed the button to recline Cosette's chair fully and tucked the blanket around her.

She blinked up at him. "Maybe a kiss good night would help," she said.

Isaac chuckled. "Worth trying." He placed his hands on either side of her abdomen, leaned in, and kissed her. He was going to keep it soft and short, but she gripped his shirt in her fists and pulled him in tighter. Isaac had no problem complying. If kissing was what she needed, he would happily take care of her need. He'd kissed a variety of women, but nothing felt like kissing Cosette. It filled him with a natural buzz of energy and warmth while making him dream of never having to stop or be apart.

When the kiss ended, he settled in next to her and reclined his chair, pulling a blanket over himself. Reaching out his hand, he clasped hers. He found that he was actually feeling sleepy. Hopefully, that stuff would work. He'd be fine without sleep, but it was always better to be fully rested. And he was anxious about whatever they were getting into. The FBI assured him they'd have people all around, ready to swoop in and arrest Lansky as soon as Blaine was safe. Still, he felt uneasy. Sometimes he felt these stirrings before a mission, but he had men he trusted around him during those times, and right now he didn't want the woman he loved walking into danger. He had to keep her safe at all costs, and that could easily distract him from the larger mission.

"Ike?" Cosette's voice sounded sleepy and sweet. He liked when she used that nickname.

"Yeah?"

"I'm scared."

He rubbed his thumb along the back of her hand. "Don't be, love. I'm here."

"But what if he cuts you up?" Her voice trembled.

"It won't happen. I hate to be the one to brag about this to you." He put a cocky note in his voice. "But your man is tougher than a dozen of Lansky's cronies."

She laughed, but it sounded unsteady. Her free hand moved over to rest on his chest, and she leaned her head against his shoulder. "I love you."

Isaac cupped her hand with his own and kissed her forehead. "I love you."

Neither of them said anything else, but within minutes, she

was breathing evenly. Isaac felt the overwhelming responsibility of rescuing her father and keeping her safe. Lansky hurting Isaac? He rolled his eyes. Not even in the cards.

Isaac startled awake as the plane touched down in San Francisco. Cosette was breathing deeply and no longer clinging to his hand, though one of her hands was still on his abdomen. He looked over her face, innocent and perfect in rest. His stomach tightened with the resolve to protect her.

Peering out the windows, he saw that the sky was just turning pink. They taxied for a while to the spot where private jets and charters were sent to disembark. As the plane slowed and stopped, he wasn't sure he wanted to wake Cosette up. They would have a long day of waiting until ten p.m.

A few minutes later, the cockpit door opened. Isaac liked that it was only Joshua's pilot who flew with them, not a stewardess or flight crew. Noticing that Cosette still sleeping, the guy whispered, "I'm going to get some food. You're welcome to stay as long as you want."

"Thanks," Isaac murmured.

"Joshua asked me to fly you to Florida on Sunday as well, so just text or call me when you're wanting to go."

"Thanks," Isaac repeated, though his gut clenched.

The pilot opened the door and left, shutting it behind him.

Cosette slept on. Isaac studied her beautiful face. Sunday. Today was Friday. He would leave her in two days. That was more upsetting than going to face Lansky and his losers.

Half an hour later, the sun peeked through the windows and Cosette stirred.

"Hello, sleeping beauty," he said.

She smiled up at him, her eyes still full of sleep. Stretching, she asked, "Have we been on the ground long?"

"Only a few hours."

"What?" She scrambled out of the recliner, which wasn't an easy feat as it was still fully reclined.

Isaac laughed and pushed his button to drop the legs on his chair, then did the same for hers. He stood and opened his arms. "Sorry. I shouldn't tease you. It's not even seven a.m."

She walked into his arms and hugged him tight. "Normally, I love to be teased, especially by you, but I'm a mess right now."

"I understand. What can I do to help? Besides not teasing."

"You're doing it." She cuddled in against him, and Isaac savored her firm body and her sweet smell. He could do this all day long. Unfortunately, they had to face her crazy, mafia-affiliated ex tonight. After that was over, they would have to figure out how to make a long-distance relationship work.

There was no other option. Now that he knew what it felt like to be with Cosette, he couldn't go back.

CHAPTER TWELVE

Cosette fidgeted, shifting her weight from foot to foot as she clung to Isaac's hand. They were on the edge of Pier 32, right next to the water. It smelled like wet cement, mold, and garbage. It was ten p.m., and there was no sign of Vance or his men yet. Her stomach was tied in knots, and even though it was a crisp February night with that bay breeze slicing right through her, she had sweat dripping between her breasts. She hoped her perfume was holding up, then scolded herself for such a silly thought. She should be hoping she wasn't interfering with the tracking device in her bra by sweating so profusely. What did sweat and moisture do to tracking devices? Who knew? Maybe Isaac knew. She didn't know if she should ask him right now. He seemed pretty intense and focused—more the Military Isaac than the Loving Cosette Isaac.

The FBI had met with them after lunch and got them outfitted with tracking devices, one hidden in the waistband of their pants, one hidden in her bra, and one inside Isaac's jacket.

The FBI was also crawling around this pier. As soon as Vance showed up with her dad, they would pounce, and as long as nobody got shot, they'd all walk away from here soon. It had been a miserable day worrying about her dad. Even though he annoyed her sometimes with his overprotectiveness, and she agreed with Mar that he should trust her more, he really was all the family she had left, and she loved him.

Luckily, Isaac was strong and unafraid. Cosette had to trust that he would take care of her and rescue her dad. His gaze was darting around, and she could tell he was listening intently. He glanced down at her. "You okay?"

She nodded, hoping that the jerky movement came across as serious rather than nervous.

Isaac squeezed her hand, but his eyes were on the shadows of the warehouse next to them, on the walkways, and even down in the water.

"What are you looking for?" Cosette whispered.

Isaac took a slow breath. "Anything." He edged toward the water and peered more closely at it.

Cosette looked down too. The water looked a freezing dark gray, and she shivered. Then she saw what Isaac was staring at with a furrowed brow. There were bubbles coming up. What could be making those bubbles? Her stomach rolled with an irrational fear. Was someone down there? She backed instinctively away.

Suddenly, the warehouse door behind them burst open and footsteps pounded their way. Cosette whirled to see who was coming. Isaac dodged in front of her, shielding her. The men were black dots in the night. As they came out of the shadows, she saw why: they were wearing black wetsuits with tight black hoods over their heads.

She clung to Isaac's back, peering around his shoulder.

The men's faces showed no expression as they ran straight at them. Isaac grabbed the first one and shoved him off the dock and into the water. The man let out a surprised yelp. The second guy was right behind, but Isaac threw solid punches at him and drove him back.

As the third guy joined the fray, Isaac was a wonder with fists and kicks, fighting both of them at once. She'd never been so impressed, nor had she appreciated violence so thoroughly.

The fourth man dodged around the brawl, grabbed Cosette, and threw her and himself off the dock.

"Ike!" Cosette screamed in horror as she hit the icy cold water. Her skin felt like it had been submerged in an ice bath. The water felt heavy and so cold she couldn't even breathe, which she realized was a good thing. She closed her mouth but wondered how quickly she'd drown, as the man had a hold of her arm and was pulling her farther under. Even with her eyes open, she couldn't see anything but bodies plunging around her in the water. Was Isaac being drowned too? Why would Vance go to such elaborate lengths to kill them? Who cared? She was going to suffocate or freeze to death.

A man in full scuba gear approached and shoved a regulator into her mouth. She clamped down on it and sucked in a breath, but there was salt water in it too. Sputtering and coughing, she was even more certain she was going to drown. She tried to expel the water, blowing out hard. Her next breath was blessedly free of water and filled her lungs.

Frozen clear through, she tried to see through the dark, murky water. The man had an iron grip on her arm, and suddenly they shot forward through the water. She had no clue what was pulling them forward. Her feet and hands were so numb, they felt like they would break off as she was dragged away from any hope of rescue.

Squeezing her eyes shut, all she could do was keep taking breaths in and out, and pray.

Cosette heard voices around her and could smell metal, sweaty men, dust, and Isaac. He was close. Her eyelids were so heavy, but she tried to pry them open. It didn't work. She remembered being propelled through the cold water and then being yanked onto a boat, wrapped up in a blanket, and someone coming at her with a needle. Considering how cloudy her brain felt, they must've drugged her. Her clothes weren't even damp, and she was only slightly chilled. How much time had passed? How had they gotten ... wherever they were?

"Cozy?" Isaac's voice was right at her ear.

She tried harder to open her eyes, squinting at him. He gave her a reassuring smile but didn't touch her. She tried to move to touch him but realized her hands were tied behind her back—maybe by zip ties, as they felt like plastic and dug into her wrists. They were both sitting against a wall. She was leaning heavily into Isaac.

"Where are we?" she whispered.

"They're awake!" a man yelled, and Cosette startled.

Yanking her gaze from Isaac's handsome face, she looked around at a large warehouse, the sides of the open main room stacked with shipping containers. It was dimly lit with the exterior doors closed. She could see another body across the open space. Was that? It couldn't be ... "Dad!" she screamed, struggling to her feet.

Isaac helped her up and then pushed off the wall and stood next to her. She started toward her dad, but several men walked out of a hallway and she shuffled backward, not wanting to be anywhere near the man in the middle. She pressed against Isaac's chest. He was a steadying influence, even though he couldn't hold her.

"Cosette." Vance spread his hands, grinning broadly. That face she'd once thought was appealing now looked cruel and too thin. "My mad scientist. So glad you came to see me."

Three more men came down the hallway and flanked him. There were six so far, including Vance. Could Isaac really fight so many? Not with his hands behind his back. Her stomach rolled, and she could only pray that their tracking devices hadn't been ruined in that cold water.

Cosette glared at him but had to ask, "My dad?"

"Oh, he's fine. We've had him pretty sleepy."

"Did you hurt him?" she demanded.

Vance shook his head. "What kind of a monster do you think I am? I wouldn't hurt an old man."

She didn't believe him. "Where are we? What do you want?"

"Now slow down, doll."

Isaac's body tightened behind her. Cosette's heart was beating faster and faster. Her gaze darted around the men. They all looked tough, brutish. One guy stood out to her. He had a handsome though seasoned face and was extremely muscular. His arms were covered in tattoos; she could even see tattoos peeking out of the top of his T-shirt and climbing his neck. Yet he didn't look as mean as the others. On the contrary, she could've sworn he gave her a kind smile. No. It was probably more of a leer. Even in this situation, she was too trusting.

"One question at a time," Vance said. "We're just west of the Las Vegas strip."

He paused to let that sink in. So they'd knocked them out and transported them to Las Vegas while they slept. She felt disoriented but even more terrified. Could the FBI have followed them here?

As if he'd guessed her thoughts, Vance smiled. "Don't worry about the FBI finding you. We removed all your tracking devices before we left San Francisco." His voice lowered, and he swept his gaze over her and winked. "All of them, doll."

Cosette's stomach squirmed, but she tilted her chin up imperiously. She still had her bra on, so they must have had to ... Ew. She couldn't let her overactive imagination get away with her on this one. *Focus on Isaac. Focus on Isaac.*

"And as to what I want ..." Vance walked closer. She was afraid he would touch her, but he glanced at Isaac and stopped a couple of feet away. "I want you, doll."

Isaac let out a growl that made Vance step back toward his men.

Yet Vance's cocky attitude didn't stop. "We both know you're socially inept, crazy as a redhead, and horrible at making love ..."

Isaac's body went even stiffer against hers. Cosette grimaced, and she wanted to assure Isaac that she'd never been like that with Vance, but now was not the time.

"Don't you dare," Isaac growled.

Vance took another step back. He focused on Cosette as if he were trying to ignore Isaac. "But you're beautiful, you make me laugh, you're the only woman who's ever escaped me ..." He winked as if this were all some game, but his voice trembled slightly. Isaac unnerved him, even with all of Vance's manpower and Isaac's hands bound. "And I want your money, of course."

"I'll give you all my money," she said quickly. "Just let us go."

He grinned, but his gaze flickered to Isaac and she could read the uncertainty there. "I'm afraid it doesn't work like that. You hurt me, doll. You're never leaving me again, and now someone has to pay for your sins." He gestured with his chin.

All five of his men sprang into action. One of them pulled Cosette away from Isaac. The other four grabbed Isaac and manhandled him to his knees. With his hands behind his back, Isaac couldn't fight them. How could he fight four men anyway?

"Ike!" she screamed out.

He glanced up at her. His blue eyes were somber but determined. He looked so strong, despite the position he was in. Two of the guys stayed on the floor next to Isaac, one on each side holding him in place. The other two stood close by, ready to help restrain him if needed.

Bile rose in Cosette's throat as she imagined what was coming. "Vance, no," she begged, horror rushing through her. "Please, no. I'll stay with you. I'll give you all my money. I'll do anything. Please don't hurt him."

Vance pulled out a knife and smiled as he walked slowly toward Isaac. "Thank you, doll. I wanted to know what the stiff military dude meant to you. Obviously a lot, and obviously I need to teach him who's in charge."

Cosette whimpered and tried to pull free, but the guy had her in a vice grip.

Vance reached Isaac. He lifted Isaac's shirt and sliced through it easily, demonstrating how sharp the knife was.

Isaac glared up at him, unafraid. "Very soon I'm going to rip your arms off, and then you're going to apologize to Cosette."

Vance drew back, fear tracing across his face. Then he looked at his men and laughed. They all chuckled with him. "I don't think you're in any position to be making threats," he said.

Isaac raised his eyebrows. The muscles in his back and arms popped with his hands behind his back. Cosette admired his bravery, but she knew that Vance was right. He had all the power here, and he enjoyed hurting people. How could she let him hurt Isaac? Her breath came in shorts pants, and her body trembled.

"Vance." Cosette tried to make her voice commanding. "Stop!" She scrambled for some way to make him stop, as he didn't even glance her direction. "Isaac's family is rich. You can have all my money and even more money from them, but only if you don't hurt him."

Vance finally looked at her, but it was only to give her a cocky tilt of his eyebrows and say, "Don't worry. I'll get every drop of money out of both of you. After I take some drops of his blood." His face became savage as he angled the knife toward Isaac's back.

"No!" Cosette screamed, flailing to get away from her captor.

Isaac's hands burst free of their restraints, and he grabbed the man on his left and rolled with him. The guy screamed as he was shoved into the knife, shoulder first. As they rolled, they toppled Vance and the other brute. Blood spattered Vance from the man's shoulder wound, and he yelped.

Isaac scrambled to his feet. Cosette worried that the other two men would come at him and he'd be fighting six on one, but miraculously, the tattooed guy she'd noticed earlier turned, grabbed the guy next to him, and tossed him against the nearest container. The man screamed in surprise as he hit the container and then the concrete.

The tattooed guy ran to face the other men, side by side with Isaac, as Vance and the other two men disentangled themselves and stood. The guy with the knife in his shoulder looked more enraged than hurt. He yanked the knife free and waved it dangerously at Isaac and Tattoo Guy. "Traitor," he sneered.

Tattoo Guy gestured to him. "Come on, scum, let's go."

Vance backed away as the other four started battling it out. The man who'd hit the container staggered to his feet and hurried toward the fray. The guy holding Cosette knocked her feet out from under her and threw her to the ground. She hit face-first and cried out in pain and surprise.

"Cozy!" Isaac yelled, and she heard bodies hit the concrete.

She could hear the fight going strong, and her nose was assaulted by the stenches of sweat, blood, and men. Yet she could also smell Isaac.

He lifted her easily to her feet. "You're okay?"

"Yes ... Ike!" she gasped. A man was coming at him from behind.

Isaac turned and deflected the punch coming at him with his forearm, then slammed his fists into the man's body. With his shirt cut away from his back, Cosette watched in awe as the muscles of his back rippled while he threw punch after punch, fighting two men at once. Tattoo Guy was definitely an asset, as he also fought two men. One of Vance's guys was splayed facedown on the concrete, unconscious.

One of the guys fighting Isaac jabbed at him. Isaac grabbed the man's arm and whipped him around. The sickening sound of bone breaking was drowned out by the man's wail. Isaac released his arm and put him in a choke hold. The man flailed and dug at Isaac's arm with his unbroken arm, but Isaac held strong, using the man's body to shield himself from the other guy who was trying to hit at him. The man in the choke hold finally went slack. Isaac tossed him away and started pummeling the other man with hits and kicks.

"Yes!" Cosette cheered.

Arms wrapped around her waist and yanked her backward.

"No!" she screamed. Her hands were useless pinned behind her, but she flailed and tried to kick at her captor. "Ike!"

"Shut up," Vance growled in her ear.

"Isaac!" she screamed louder.

Isaac turned to her, and his eyes widened. He grabbed the man he was fighting and slammed him down to the concrete, then sprinted toward her and Vance.

Cosette dug her heels in and slammed her head back into Vance's. He yelped in pain, and his grip on her loosened. Isaac reached them, grabbed Vance, and hauled him away from Cosette.

Vance's eyes were wide with fear as Isaac glowered down at him.

"Now," Isaac said in a low, dangerous voice. "Let me show you how it feels to have your arms ripped off."

"Please," Vance begged, cowering. "Don't hurt me."

Isaac glanced at Cosette. "You really dated this loser?"

Cosette let out a shaky laugh. "I was being an idiot. Forgive me?"

He grinned. "Always." He glowered back at Vance. "Now about that apology."

Sirens cut through the air, and Vance's face turned white. One of the men Tattoo Guy was fighting broke free and sprinted for an exit door. Tattoo Guy clocked the other man in the temple. He went down hard, and Tattoo Guy took off after the sprinting man.

"Ike, my dad." Cosette didn't care about Vance apologizing.

She only cared that her dad and Isaac were okay and that Vance was arrested.

Isaac dragged Vance toward the corner where her father lay. Cosette shuffled behind them.

"If he's hurt, I will use that knife to carve you up," Isaac said, "before I rip your arms off."

"Please, I can pay you," Vance whimpered.

Isaac let out a menacing growl, and Vance clammed up.

Cosette hurried to the corner. It was awkward to run with her hands behind her back. Police poured in through an open man door, infiltrated the warehouse, and started yelling for everybody to put their hands up. Ignoring them, she dropped to her knees next to her dad. Her eyes scanned the length of his body, and she let out a sigh of relief. He didn't look cut or beaten up, just curled up as if he were sleeping. She bent her head down and put her cheek next to his nose. She could feel his soft, warm exhalation on her cheek and breathed out, "Oh, thank you, Lord."

She glanced up at Isaac, who had shoved Vance at a police officer and now dropped to his knees next to her. "He's breathing," she said.

He smiled reassuringly and put his fingers to her dad's neck for a few seconds before saying, "Pulse is strong."

Cosette leaned against Isaac, and he wrapped his free arm around her. "Thank you," she whispered. "You were so brave."

He smiled. "When I felt that my zip ties were partially cut, I knew I had somebody willing to help me. Luckily, the guy with the tattoos was on our side. He was tough."

"Not as tough as you."

Isaac leaned close to kiss her, but a man yelled right behind them. "Police! Get your hands up!"

Isaac stood to face him and helped Cosette up. The guy's eyes flickered from Cosette with her hands bound behind her back, to Isaac looking so strong and fearsome with his shirt cut and some scrapes on his face and arms.

"We're the people who were kidnapped last night," Isaac explained slowly. "Isaac Jewel and Cosette Peterson." He gestured toward the floor with his chin. "That's Blaine Peterson. He needs an ambulance."

The guy lowered his gun slightly and spoke into a radio extension at his shoulder, still watching Isaac uneasily.

Tattoo Guy came striding across the open area, talking and laughing with an older gentleman who looked important. He saw them, said something to the other man, and they both headed their direction. "They're with me," Tattoo Guy said. "Can you please cut her loose?"

The policeman didn't say anything but stowed his gun and readily complied, pulling out a knife and cutting the zip ties. Cosette rubbed at her wrists.

The important-looking guy slapped Tattoo Guy on the shoulder. "Sorry you blew your cover, but I think we'll get some great information with the computers here and the men we've arrested." He smiled kindly at Cosette and walked away.

Tattoo Guy's smile split his handsome face. He reminded her of Mel Gibson in *Braveheart*, sans long hair but adding in the myriad of tattoos.

Isaac extended his hand. "I'm also sorry you blew your cover, but I will be forever grateful for the help."

"I couldn't let that weasel torture you."

"Who are you?" Cosette asked.

His smile broadened. "Jesse Panetto. My family and I have been battling human trafficking for over ten years now."

"Jesse." She shook his hand. "Good, I can stop thinking of you as Tattoo Guy."

Jesse threw his head back and laughed. "My wife called me Dr. Tattoo when she first met me."

"You're a doctor too?"

"Yes, ma'am."

"Can you ...?" She pointed at her dad.

"Of course. Sorry, I got distracted." He dropped to his knees and checked her dad's vitals as well as his spine. "I didn't notice anyone hurting him, but you never know with these losers," he muttered.

Isaac wrapped his arm around her, and Cosette leaned heavily into his side.

Finally, Jesse looked up. "He's been heavily drugged, but I can't find any damage. Of course, the hospital can run tests to make certain there's no internal damage."

She shuddered and glanced up at Isaac. "If there's internal damage, I'll support you ripping Vance's arms off."

"I might rip them off anyway for him belittling you."

Cosette felt a warm current rush through her. Isaac was so protective and good.

Jesse stood and looked at Cosette. "You remind me of my wife: beautiful, feisty, and no filter. Speaking of my wife ... Since you blew my cover, I'm headed home to my wife and boys." He grinned even bigger and saluted them. "I wish you two every happiness." Then he was gone.

Cosette turned to Isaac, cuddling against his chest. Her arms wrapped around his back, and she startled as they met bare skin. It was weird how she'd forgotten, as she'd watched Vance cut his shirt, but she'd tried to push that image away. A shudder raced through her, and tears pricked at her eyes. "He didn't hurt you. I was so scared."

Isaac tilted up her chin, a cocky smile on his face. "That wimp couldn't have hurt me."

"You'd rip his arms off?"

"Dang the police for interrupting before I could follow through on that one."

Cosette shuddered again.

Isaac chuckled and framed her face with his hands. "I won't rip anybody's arms off. I'd rather be kissing you anyway." Lowering his head, he followed through with that promise.

Cosette clung to him and returned each kiss. The horror of the past who knew how many hours disappeared as she relished being in Isaac's arms, safe, warm, and loved. If only she knew he wouldn't be leaving her soon.

CHAPTER THIRTEEN

Isaac had to let Cosette go as the Vegas police took them into the station and separated them for questioning. It was late Saturday afternoon when they were finally released. He was starving and tired and ready to eat and then hold Cosette close and sleep, but they decided first to go see her father at the hospital.

Blaine was asleep when they got there. Cosette stood by his bedside and took his hand. Tears slid down her face, and Isaac knew she was reliving the nightmare of almost losing him. Isaac didn't know what to do besides stand close by and wrap his arm around her waist. She leaned into him, and it made him feel like the king of the world. How was he going to leave her tomorrow?

They didn't speak or move for a while as she held her dad's hand and Isaac kept her close. Finally, her dad stirred and then opened his eyes. He blinked up at Cosette, and then his gaze shifted to Isaac. Isaac wondered briefly if he should step away, but he refused to. He wasn't a teenager, and he refused to hide his love for Cosette from her dad.

Her dad's face cracked into a smile. "Look at the two of you," he murmured.

Cosette squeezed his hand. "Are you all right? Can I get you anything?"

He waved his other hand. "The nurses came in earlier and got me all comfortable and gave me a drink. I just want to look at you, my beautiful girl. Are you all right?"

"Yes." She smiled worshipfully up at Isaac. "Thanks to Isaac."

Isaac returned her smile.

"Yes, I hear we owe a lot to Isaac. One of the nurses relayed the entire story. Apparently she heard it from the paramedics that came for me, who heard it from the police ..." He chuckled dryly. "Thank you, Isaac," he murmured. "Thank you for rescuing both of us."

Isaac nodded. "I'd do anything for Cosette, sir."

Her dad's eyebrow arched up. "Anything?"

Cosette stiffened in his arms, and Isaac was very concerned where Blaine was going to lead him.

"Leave the military?"

Cosette sucked in a breath. "Dad ... I appreciate you always being concerned about me, but I'm an adult now. Isaac and I will work this out on our own."

Her dad's eyebrows lifted. "I'm sorry I'm so overprotective."

She shrugged. "I love you being there for me, but you need to trust me also. I'm not a flighty teenager anymore."

He nodded. "I do trust you, and I love you very much. I apologize, love. I'm just a man, and without your mother around, I don't understand girls very well."

"Women," Isaac corrected, his eyebrows tilting in a warning.

Cosette smiled at him.

"I'm with you on the not understanding *women*, sir," Isaac commiserated.

Blaine chuckled. "Okay, my little girl's a woman. Don't rub it in."

The subject changed back to the kidnapping and rescue, and Cosette told him all about Tattoo Guy and how tough Isaac was. Isaac listened and smiled and commented, but his mind was scrambling to figure out how to be with Cosette. He wasn't leaving the Air Force. His team needed him. He was proud to be serving his country, and he lived to be part of the action, fighting and protecting others.

Yet leaving her might rip him in two. His grip tightened around Cosette. Why did life have to be so hard?

Cosette watched Isaac's profile as they sat at a table in their suite at the MGM Grand that night and ate through several orders of room service. She'd ordered a raspberry-chicken salad. Isaac had ordered steak and shrimp with a baked potato, veggies, a roll, a salad, and a side of a full chicken alfredo entrée with an entire cake for dessert.

She smiled as she watched him eat, smelling the hearty flavor of the steak. She'd loved cooking for him at their protected beach bungalow in Vieques. That time seemed far away. Even though Isaac was still right here with her, he felt far away as well. Like she was already losing him.

He ate several bites of cake and then sat back. "Sorry if I acted like a pig. I was starved."

She smiled. "I'll tell your mom you still showed very good manners, even starved."

"Thank you." Isaac stood, and she helped him pile all of the empty and half-empty plates onto the tray. He made an exception for the cake, which he carried over to the small counter. When he returned from taking the tray into the hallway, he extended his hand and looked at her very seriously. "Can we talk?"

She pulled a face. "The dreaded talk."

"Followed by lots of amazing kissing," he promised.

She smiled. "Oh? I guess talking might be worth it then." She clasped his hand, and he pulled her up. They walked together over to the section of couches that looked out over the Vegas strip. "I hate this city," she murmured, settling into the couch next to Isaac.

"Because of Vance?" he asked, leaning against the cushion to face her.

She turned to look at him as well, wishing he was simply holding her. "Mostly, but also ..." She gestured out. "It's all fake. Fake New York, fake pyramid, fake Eiffel Tower ... Did you know they even have a fake beach?"

"You have an issue with fake. Noted." Isaac smiled gently.

She placed her hand in his, marveling at how right it felt. Could he truly just leave her?

"I want to tell you something, Cozy."

"Shoot," she said.

He looked straight into her eyes and said, "Lansky is an idiot. You never told me details, but I can gather from the few demeaning things he said this morning that he belittled and berated you."

Cosette might've preferred talking about how Isaac was leaving her. She nodded. "When we first met in Italy, it was all romance and roses. Then we both returned to the States and our relationship was mostly FaceTime and text and email, which was fine by me, as I was busy with work. He came to San Francisco for Christmas and proposed and was still as fake and sweet as ever. Of course, I bought it. When he flew me to Vegas to be with him ..." Her voice trailed off and she looked out the window, then said in a harsh whisper, "I never slept with him. You believe me, right?"

"Oh, Cozy." Isaac drew her close and kissed her softly. "There's no way someone with the innocent light in your eyes could've slept with a loser like that. I definitely believe you."

"Thanks." She studied their clasped hands as she rushed out the rest of the stupid story. She didn't need to worry about Vance anymore, but she wanted to trust and share with Isaac. "When I came here at first, it was like Italy again, all romantic as he made all kinds of inflated promises. Then he started finding fault with everything I said, wore, did, how I kissed ..." She cringed at the murderous look on Isaac's face. "After less than a week, I'd had enough. I don't have much experience or confidence with men, but I knew I deserved better than that. Mar thinks he was trying to tear me down so he could manipulate me into moving here and steal my money." She shook her head.

"Anyway," she started again, "I was going to tell him we were through. I had a key to his suite, so I just let myself in. That's when I saw him torturing that man. The guy was screaming loud enough—" She cringed. "—I was able to escape before anyone saw me. Then the belittlement just got worse through texts when he realized I was gone, until I blocked him. You're right: he's an idiot. He thought tearing me down would make me think I wasn't worthy of anything more and I'd come back to him."

Isaac tilted up her chin with his palm. "You need to know that he lied about all of it."

"What do you mean?"

"The way you dress is beautiful and refreshing, the way you talk is hilarious and intriguing, and the way you kiss ..." He blew out a breath and gave her a smoldering look that she felt down to her toes. "Kissing you is the best time of my life."

Cosette wanted to cry at his sweet words. Instead, she lifted herself onto his lap, wrapped her arms around his neck, and kissed him. He pulled her in tight and proceeded to back up his beautiful statements with a desire and love for her that blew away all of Vance's belittlement like sand in a windstorm.

As the kisses slowed down, he held her close. "Are you tired?" he asked.

"Yes," she admitted, but she didn't want this night to end.

"Can I ... hold you tonight?"

Cosette stared at him. Did he think that she would compromise her values because he was leaving? That didn't seem like the Isaac she knew, or like his background and family.

"Cozy," he said, and there was laughter in his voice. "Just hold you. I promise I'll keep your virtue safe."

She smiled. "It's all on you, then. If I attack you in the night, you'll have to resist me."

"Maybe this isn't such a good idea."

She pushed herself to her feet. "I won't attack you, wussy military man."

"Did you just call me a wuss?"

"Yes, I did." She tossed her hair.

Isaac jumped to his feet and scooped her off the ground, tossing her over his shoulder. Cosette squealed and laughed as he ran for the master bedroom and she bounced on his shoulder. He dumped her onto the bed, then proceeded to tickle her.

"Stop," she begged, pushing at his hands but unable to budge him one inch. "Stop!"

"Take it back." He held his hands poised over her stomach, and he lifted his eyebrows.

She giggled. "I'm sorry. You're the toughest man I know."

"That's better." He laughed with her, but then his gaze swept over her and his laughter faded.

He lowered himself onto the bed and kissed her more thoroughly than she'd ever been kissed. When he pulled back, they were both breathing heavily, and Cosette was so stirred up she had no desire for sleep anymore.

"Okay," Isaac said in a gruff voice. "This obviously isn't going to work."

He started to push himself up, but Cosette grabbed at his shirt. "Please," she murmured. She wanted to remind him that he was leaving her in the morning, but his blue eyes told her that he didn't need that reminder—he was as torn up inside as she was.

Isaac drew in a heavy breath and said, "Here's how tonight is going to play out, and don't challenge me on this," he warned.

Cosette smiled. "I wouldn't dream of it."

He slid off the bed and turned it down. "You go in there."

She obediently slid into the covers. He tucked them over her, then lay down next to her, adjusting the pillow under his head and wrapping his arm across her abdomen. It wasn't nearly enough contact for her, but she knew they were playing with fire staying so close throughout the night. She'd take what she could get.

A sobering thought hit her as they lay there. Would she ever get enough of Isaac, or would she always be longing for more?

The next morning, time flew by far too quickly. Isaac wanted to talk through their relationship and their future, but it never came up at breakfast or as they drove to the airport. What was he going to say, anyway?

The car pulled up to the Henderson Executive Airport. Isaac did like the convenience of flying in his brother's jet, especially when they didn't use the international airport and he didn't have to waste time going through security. He wanted to have a minute alone with Cosette, not with crowds of people walking past.

They unloaded not too far from the jet. The driver handed Isaac his bag, and Isaac asked him to please wait to take the lady back to her hotel. She was going to stay with her dad until he was released from the hospital, and then she'd fly back to San Francisco with him. Isaac handed the guy a credit card to pay for both trips and palmed him some extra tip money.

"Thanks, man. I'll be in the car." He gave Isaac a wink. "Don't worry, I'll be playing Clash of Clans on my phone and won't be looking."

Isaac grinned. "Thanks."

He headed toward the plane with Cosette walking quietly beside him. Dropping his bag next to the steps that led into the plane, he turned to her. Her lower lip was trembling, and he felt awful about it. She gave a little whimper and then threw herself at him. Isaac caught her easily and held her tight.

"We never got the chance to talk about ... us," he said.

Cosette looked up at him. "As in our long-distance relationship?"

"Yeah." His hands tightened on her waist as he tried to memorize every freckle on her perfect nose, the cute way she talked, the way her hair smelled, and how it felt to have her close. "I *hate* this."

"When's your next leave?"

"Two months," he grunted out, wanting to go AWOL for the first time in his eleven-year career with the Air Force.

"Do you get days off, like on the weekend?"

"When I'm not deployed or we don't get called out on a mission."

"Well, if that happens, I'll fly to you."

"Thank you," he managed to say; his throat was suddenly thick. He tugged her closer and kissed her. "I just don't want to leave you. I feel like it's all going to fall apart if we're not together."

She wrinkled her nose at him. "O ye of little faith. You might stink at long-distance relationships, but look how well my last one turned out."

He choked on a bitter laugh, realizing she meant the nightmare with Lansky.

She winked but then framed his face with her hands. "I love you, Isaac. It's going to be tough, but we'll make it work ... somehow."

Isaac didn't have any words to make it better. He kissed her instead. He kissed her desperately and clung to her, wanting her to know for certain that he loved her too. Truly, though, he couldn't see how this would work out. Not with her in San Francisco and him in Florida, or any other undisclosed location in the world.

The pilot approached from the hangar, and Isaac drew back.

"Forgive me, sir," the pilot said.

"You're fine," Isaac reassured him, though none of this was fine.

Cosette kissed him one more time, then stepped back. "I love you," she said.

"I love you," he repeated fiercely, hoping she could read it all over his face. He'd never known love like this, and it was worth fighting for, worth waiting for. If only there was some end in sight.

She lifted a hand, but then her face crumpled and she turned and ran for the taxi.

Isaac waited until she was inside before hefting his bag and walking on the plane. He felt like each of his shoes was a concrete block that weighed dozens of pounds. He'd fought terrorists and people who wanted to kill him all over the world, but nothing was as heavy and awful as this. Leaving her was the hardest thing he'd ever done.

CHAPTER FOURTEEN

The month after Isaac left was misery. March came without any hope of their situation changing. Cosette kept herself very busy in her lab, and in her free time she talked to Isaac through FaceTime every chance they had. Sometimes it was fun to talk to him, but sometimes he was withdrawn or distracted, and she feared they were just drawing further apart.

The rest of the time, she ran, cooked, baked, and spent time with Mar and her dad. She was sadly grounded in reality. Her imagination barely worked well enough to create new scents. Last weekend, she'd been able to fly to Isaac and spend a blissful day with him on Destin Beach near his base, but then she'd had to walk away from him again, and it was worse than the last time. Unless one of them was willing to budge on their careers, she didn't see an end in sight.

Isaac had leave coming up in five weeks, so they were trying to decide where to spend the week together. She wouldn't mind going back to their little house on that little island off of Puerto

Rico, but unless they impulsively got married, it probably wasn't too smart to be alone like that for a week. Not with how heated and intense their kissing sessions were when they were together.

Her lab door burst open, and she looked up in surprise. She worked pretty much in seclusion, sending off her final products for testing and then production to the facility attached to the lab that she and Mar owned. She knew people were right there, but they rarely bugged her.

Mar stormed in, looking perfect as ever in a fitted pale blue blouse and a multi-patterned pencil skirt, her five-inch heels making her almost five-four. No matter how small Mar was, she was in charge of the world. She flipped her long, dark hair and narrowed her eyes at Cosette. "I'm your best friend, right?"

"Well, yeah."

"Since how long?" She arched a perfectly plucked eyebrow. She plucked Cosette's eyebrows too, when Cosette let her.

"Since middle school when you beat up Melissa Oliver for making fun of me. Why?" Cosette set down her test tube and stood and stretched.

"I'm done with you mooning over Isaac Jewel."

Cosette's eyes widened and she felt fire rise up in her. "Well, sorry about that." She drew out the phrase sarcastically. "But I will never be done with Isaac Jewel."

Mar folded her arms over her perfect bosom and rolled her eyes. "Lord give me strength. I didn't say you were done with Isaac; I said you were done with mooning over him."

"Hallelujah. I'd love to figure out how to be together. What's the solution, my genie?"

Mar smiled and beckoned to someone who must have been just outside the door. Her dad walked in with ... Rachel Jewel?

Cosette stepped back. "Rachel?"

"Hi, Cosette." She grinned brightly and pressed her hands together. Her bright blue Jewel eyes made Cosette miss Isaac all the more. "Mar called me, and I think the plan is brilliant."

"What plan?" Cosette looked from Rachel to Mar to her dad. She wasn't even aware that Mar knew Rachel. "You're in on this?" she asked her dad. He'd recovered from the drugs Vance's men had pumped into him, and Vance was still in prison awaiting trial for a variety of crimes. Her relationship with her dad was better than ever. They enjoyed being together, and he hardly ever treated her like a child.

Her dad gave her two thumbs-up. "I just helped orchestrate a few things. So, we flying to Florida?"

Cosette gripped the back of a chair. "Florida? But Isaac only has one day off this weekend. His next leave isn't for five weeks."

"'O ye of little faith,'" her dad quoted, reminding her of her mom.

Cosette felt the spark of excitement. "You're all going to help me be with Isaac?"

Rachel nodded. "And for longer than just a day, or a week. It just requires you being a little brave. Are you brave, Cosette?"

Cosette pulled a face. No, she wasn't anything like Isaac as far as bravery went. She wanted to ask for details, but she said a quick prayer and then pumped both of her fists in the air, yelling, "Let's do this!"

They all laughed and nodded at each other. "It's time," her dad said.

"It's time," Mar repeated.

Cosette wondered what it was time for.

———

Isaac walked into his house on Hurlburt Field Air Force base and slid out of his shoes. His small two-story home was nice and only a few years old. It was definitely an upgrade from when he was deployed or on an assignment and living in barracks or worse. Yet his house now felt empty, lonely, too big. Maybe he should move back to the barracks so he wasn't alone.

He walked into the kitchen in the dark. It kind of fit his mood. He tried to stay upbeat, but he was dark and lonely without Cosette. He pulled out a water bottle.

"You gonna offer me one?" a voice said from behind him.

He whipped around, ready to take out whoever dared invade his home.

A familiar chuckle reverberated through the space, and a light flipped on.

He squinted to adjust to the sudden brightness and shook his head. "Luke. I hate it when you sneak up on me. How'd you get in?"

"0858," he said, referring to the code on Isaac's front door. "Really? We all use Dad's birth month and year for all our passwords."

Isaac vowed to change his passwords to something more original. He walked over and gave his brother a brief hug. "Great to see you. How long are you here?" He had tomorrow off, so at least he'd have one day with his brother.

"Until tomorrow night." Luke clapped him on the shoulder. "C'mon. I've got to show you something."

The last thing Isaac wanted to do was go somewhere. Couldn't they just sit on the couch, chat, maybe watch some hockey? The Bruins were on tonight, and he'd always loved watching Austin Strong, even more so now that he'd met Stetson, Austin's uncle.

"Okay," he said reluctantly.

He slid back into his shoes and followed Luke outside and across the street to where Luke had parked his rented Audi. They chatted as they drove off the base and into the nearby town of Fort Walton Beach.

Pulling up to some industrial warehouse-type buildings, Luke grinned at him. "C'mon. You're going to love this."

Isaac highly doubted it. He would've loved to relax, call Cosette, and go to bed early. He forced a smile and got out of the car. Luke led the way through a regular door that was next to a huge closed bay door. They walked into a dark space. Isaac could tell that it was large from the way their footsteps echoed on the concrete floor.

"Why do I feel like Seth and Caleb are going to jump out at me any second?" he asked.

"They'll be here tomorrow," Luke said.

"Really? What for?"

"Your wedding day," the sweetest voice on the planet said from behind him.

Isaac whipped around just as a soft light haloed Cosette. His breath whooshed out, and he took a brief second to stare at her beautiful face. Rushing toward her, he picked her up and swung her around. "Cozy!" He kissed her long and hard before drawing back. "Why didn't you tell me you were coming and ..." He shook his head to clear it. "What did you just say?"

Cosette smiled up at him. "Your brothers are coming for your wedding day tomorrow."

Isaac glanced around for Luke, but he couldn't see him in the dimness stretching out from the one light that was focused on Cosette. The warehouse was a decent size, and there might have been a couple of offices or a bathroom across the open space. He focused back on what he wanted to see—Cosette.

He lowered his voice and said, "Cozy. I would marry you any day of the week, but there are a lot of questions you have to answer before that can happen." Loving and missing her so deeply had made him realize that marrying her was worth any risk, but would she think it was worth it?

"Such as?" She tilted her chin imperiously. She had the grit to be a military wife, but …

"What if I get deployed? You'll be alone for fourteen months."

"That'll suck, but I love you enough to wait for you."

He brushed the hair over her shoulder, breathing in her sweet scent. "What if I get killed?"

Cosette blinked up at him. "That'll worse than suck, but Isaac … I could get killed driving down the freeway tomorrow. We can't put our lives on hold for a what-if."

"My unit's likelihood of death is a little higher than someone driving on the freeway … Well, except for you. You are a horrible driver."

"What? I rocked that golf cart driving. And truthfully, I don't drive a car much."

Isaac chuckled but knew he had to keep going with his line of reasoning, though the thought of marrying Cosette tomorrow had him hot all over. "I don't have leave for five weeks. If we get married tomorrow, we can't even take a honeymoon."

"We worked that out," a voice called from across the open area. "General Watson owed me a favor."

"Was that your dad?" Isaac's gaze darted to the voice, but he only saw darkness and heard a deep chuckle.

Cosette nodded. "I had some help. We've got the wedding venue set, your family and some friends flying in, the honeymoon set, your leave transferred to next week ..." She shifted uneasily.

"What about living across the country from each other even when I'm not on assignment or deployed?"

"This is my future lab. Mar's going to get it ready for me while we're on our honeymoon." Cosette squeezed his hand and gestured at the large open area. "I can work from wherever you are, Ike, and Mar's found a way to ship everything safely from here to San Francisco. If you get deployed, I'll go back to San Francisco until you're done."

Isaac's eyes widened. He was reeling. Cosette would move around, set up labs and work from wherever he was? She'd do that for him? "That's very generous of you." It was lame, as he didn't really know what to say. He wanted to swoop in and propose on the spot, but he was still trying to figure all of this out.

"And *this* is very brave of me." She smiled and pushed out a shaky breath. "Ike, you know I'm a bit crazy but not really that brave. At the risk of feeling very stupid asking this question as your brother, your sister, Mar, and my dad listen in ... will you marry me?"

Isaac looked down into her beautiful face, thrilled that she'd been willing to take this step for him. He loved her and was sick and tired of being apart. If she was willing to sacrifice and set up labs close to wherever he was stationed, it would be insane to wait until a more convenient opportunity presented itself. "Yes," he murmured. "Of course, yes, my love."

There was whooping and cheering, but Isaac ignored all of

them, pulled his fiancée close, and kissed her. He wondered when they were going to get rings and where they'd go on their honeymoon and how he'd leave her again with how much he loved her, but the little details didn't matter. They loved each other, and they were going to make it work.

EPILOGUE

Cosette was amazed at what Rachel and Mar pulled together in a day. There were chairs arranged on the sand of Destin Beach and facing the ocean, and a beautiful wedding arch was covered in fresh white and pink flowers. She loved her fitted white lace dress, and as she clutched a bouquet of pale blue and pink in one hand and her father's hand in the other, she could only feel gratitude for her friend and future sister-in-law for making this happen. Cosette had never dreamt about a huge, fancy wedding. She'd only dreamt of being with Isaac.

She could see him over the heads of the seated crowd, standing tall and handsome next to his string of brothers. He stared across the people to the spot where she waited. With a beach wedding, there was nowhere for her to hide. She didn't care. She wanted Isaac to see her. He accepted and loved her, every bit.

Isaac's darling niece, Paisley, skipped down the aisle, throwing rose petals pell-mell. Everyone laughed and oohed over how cute she was. Eve went down the aisle, and Rachel followed her.

It was Mar's turn. She smacked Cosette on the rear and muttered, "Watch me wow those Jewel boys."

"All but Isaac," Cosette whispered back.

Mar winked. "Don't worry. He doesn't know another woman is alive."

Cosette laughed as Mar walked away. She noticed that Luke's gaze locked with Mar's, and it didn't look like either of them wavered. Ooh, she'd love for those two to get together.

Her dad tucked her hand through his elbow and smiled down at her. "I wish your mom could be here."

Cosette nodded, but peace washed over her. "She's here."

He studied her, then nodded as well. "You're right. You ready?"

"Yes." She'd never been more ready.

They walked sedately up the sandy aisle, her heels sinking with each step, but it didn't bother her. Nothing could bother her as she met Isaac's blue gaze, which was warm with love for her and full of promise of how their time together would be. They might not have as much time together as they wanted, but she'd savor each moment she got.

Her dad gave her away, and she kissed his cheek. She handed her bouquet off to Mar and then put both her hands in Isaac's. As she did, she felt another surge of the same warm peace of her mom was watching over their union, this time telling her that this was right. Isaac's warm hands would steady her and love her. She was safe and loved, even if she was a crazy chemist. Isaac loved her for her, especially the whimsical, funny parts, and she loved every inch of him.

DO MARRY YOUR BILLIONAIRE BOSS

A group of young men, barely out of their teens, walked past, several staring at Jade. They stopped and talked and laughed and jostled each other and kept sneaking looks at her as she slowly licked her ice cream cone. A tall redhead kid broke from the group and approached her. "Hey, pretty lady."

She smiled, having no desire to crush this young man's confidence. He was a cute kid. "Hey."

"You want to ... go for a walk?"

She tried to be nice. "That is so kind of you, but ..." But what? *I already have three men I'm interested in and you're too young to compete with any of them?*

"She has a boyfriend," said a deep, irresistible voice behind her.

Jade whirled, and there he was. Joshua looked as gorgeous as ever, wearing dark gray slacks and a button-down pale blue shirt that showed just a hint of his tanned, tough chest. His chestnut-brown hair had just that perfect wave to it, and those blue eyes yanked her right in. How she wished he truly could be her boyfriend.

"Ah, sorry, man," the guy was saying.

Joshua reached out, and she watched them shake hands. "Hey, no hard feelings. I know she's the most beautiful woman on this ship. You didn't know she was taken."

"You're one lucky dude." The kid smiled an embarrassed grin at her and then scuttled back to his friends.

Jade stared in semi-shock at Joshua as he took the chair next to her. His knees brushed hers, and he looked her over possessively as if he were her boyfriend. "You're welcome," he said.

"Excuse me?" Her temper flared up. At this point she didn't know if he could win with her, no matter what he said. What happened to him staying away until he figured out she was innocent? "What am I thanking you for?"

He smiled smoothly, and she loved that dimple. "First of all, saving you from that kid hitting on you."

She narrowed her eyes. "He seemed like a very nice young man, and I've always been partial to redheads." She folded her arms across her chest. "I don't have any problem with a cute guy hitting on me."

He edged in a little closer, and she smelled that irresistible cologne.

"Second of all ..." His voice was so irresistibly husky, it made her stomach feel all warm, like she'd just drunk a mug of hot cocoa. "You looked really lonely. I thought I'd rescue you from that."

She stood and glared down at him. "I happen to be confident enough to enjoy my own company, and I thought I explained today that you have no responsibility to protect me, watch over me, rescue me, or be around me. The only responsibility you have is to figure out who really stole your money. When you figure that out ... then you can come begging for my forgiveness. We'll see if I grant it."

———

Keep Reading here.

ABOUT THE AUTHOR

Cami is a part-time author, part-time exercise consultant, part-time housekeeper, full-time wife, and overtime mother of four adorable boys. Sleep and relaxation are fond memories. She's never been happier.

Join Cami's VIP list to find out about special deals, giveaways and new releases and receive a free copy of *Rescued by Love: Park City Firefighter Romance* by clicking here.

cami@camichecketts.com
www.camichecketts.com

ALSO BY CAMI CHECKETTS

Jewel Family Romance

Do Marry Your Billionaire Boss

Do Trust Your Special Ops Bodyguard

Do Date Your Handsome Rival

Strong Family Romance

Don't Date Your Brother's Best Friend

Her Loyal Protector

Don't Fall for a Fugitive

Her Hockey Superstar Fake Fiance

Don't Ditch a Detective

Don't Miss the Moment

Don't Love an Army Ranger

Don't Chase a Player

Don't Abandon the Superstar

Steele Family Romance

Her Dream Date Boss

The Stranded Patriot

The Committed Warrior

Extreme Devotion

Quinn Family Romance

The Devoted Groom

The Conflicted Warrior

The Gentle Patriot

The Tough Warrior

Her Too-Perfect Boss

Her Forbidden Bodyguard

Georgia Patriots Romance

The Loyal Patriot

The Gentle Patriot

The Stranded Patriot

The Pursued Patriot

Jepson Brothers Romance

How to Design Love

How to Switch a Groom

How to Lose a Fiance

Billionaire Boss Romance

Her Dream Date Boss

Her Prince Charming Boss

Hawk Brothers Romance

The Determined Groom

The Stealth Warrior

Her Billionaire Boss Fake Fiance

Risking it All

Navy Seal Romance

The Protective Warrior

The Captivating Warrior

The Stealth Warrior

The Tough Warrior

Texas Titan Romance

The Fearless Groom

The Trustworthy Groom

The Beastly Groom

The Irresistible Groom

The Determined Groom

The Devoted Groom

Billionaire Beach Romance

Caribbean Rescue

Cozumel Escape

Cancun Getaway

Trusting the Billionaire

How to Kiss a Billionaire

Onboard for Love

Shadows in the Curtain

Billionaire Bride Pact Romance

The Resilient One

The Feisty One

The Independent One

The Protective One

The Faithful One

The Daring One

Park City Firefighter Romance

Rescued by Love

Reluctant Rescue

Stone Cold Sparks

Snowed-In for Christmas

Echo Ridge Romance

Christmas Makeover

Last of the Gentlemen

My Best Man's Wedding

Change of Plans

Counterfeit Date

Snow Valley

Full Court Devotion: Christmas in Snow Valley

A Touch of Love: Summer in Snow Valley

Running from the Cowboy: Spring in Snow Valley

Light in Your Eyes: Winter in Snow Valley

Romancing the Singer: Return to Snow Valley

Fighting for Love: Return to Snow Valley

Other Books by Cami

Seeking Mr. Debonair: Jane Austen Pact

Seeking Mr. Dependable: Jane Austen Pact

Saving Sycamore Bay

Oh, Come On, Be Faithful

Protect This

Blog This

Redeem This

The Broken Path

Dead Running

Dying to Run

Fourth of July

Love & Loss

Love & Lies

Cami's Collections

Steele Family Collection

Hawk Brothers Collection

Quinn Family Collection

Cami's Military Collection

Billionaire Beach Romance Collection

Billionaire Bride Pact Collection

Billionaire Romance Sampler

Echo Ridge Romance Collection

Texas Titans Romance Collection

Snow Valley Collection

Christmas Romance Collection

Holiday Romance Collection

Extreme Sports Romance Collection

Made in United States
Cleveland, OH
15 February 2026